2061
Odyssey
Three

2061
Odyssey
Three

Arthur C. Clarke

A Del Rey Book
Ballantine Books • New York

A Del Rey Book
Published by Ballantine Books

Copyright © 1987 by Arthur C. Clarke

ISBN 1-56865-308-5

Manufactured in the United States of America

To the memory of
Judy-Lynn Del Rey,
editor extraordinary,
who bought this book for one dollar
—but never knew if she got her money's worth

Demo

Author's Note

Just as *2010: Odyssey Two* was not a direct sequel to *2001: A Space Odyssey,* so this book is not a linear sequel to *2010.* They must all be considered as variations on the same theme, involving many of the same characters and situations, but not necessarily happening in the same universe.

Developments since 1964, when Stanley Kubrick suggested (five years before men landed on the Moon!) that we should attempt "the proverbial good science-fiction movie," make total consistency impossible, as the later stories incorporate discoveries and events that had not even taken place when the earlier books were written. *2010* was made possible by the brilliantly successful 1979 Voyager flybys of Jupiter, and I had not intended to return to that territory until the results of the even more ambitious Galileo Mission were in.

Galileo would have dropped a probe into the Jovian atmosphere, while spending almost two years visiting all the major satellites. It should have been launched from the Space Shuttle in May 1986, and would have reached its objective by December 1988. So around 1990 I hoped to take advantage of the flood of new information from Jupiter and its moons . . .

Alas, the *Challenger* tragedy eliminated that scenario; Galileo—now sitting in its clean room at the Jet Propulsion Laboratory—must now find another launch vehicle. It will be lucky if it arrives at Jupiter merely seven years behind schedule.

I have decided not to wait.

Arthur C. Clarke
Colombo, Sri Lanka
April, 1987

Contents

II • THE VALLEY OF BLACK SNOW

III • EUROPAN ROULETTE

IV • AT THE WATER HOLE

V • THROUGH THE ASTEROIDS

VI • HAVEN

VII • THE GREAT WALL

VIII • THE KINGDOM OF SULFUR

IX • 3001

I
The
Magic
Mountain

1 · The Frozen Years

"For a man of seventy, you're in extremely good shape," remarked Dr. Glazunov, looking up from the Medcom's final printout. "I'd have put you down as not more than sixty-five."

"Happy to hear it, Oleg. Especially as I'm a hundred and three—as you know perfectly well."

"Here we go again! Anyone would think you've never read Professor Rudenko's book."

"Dear old Katerina! We'd planned a get-together on her hundredth birthday. I was so sorry she never made it—that's what comes of spending too much time on Earth."

"Ironic, since she was the one who coined that famous slogan 'Gravity is the bringer of old age.'"

Dr. Heywood Floyd stared thoughtfully at the ever-changing panorama of the beautiful planet, only six thousand kilometers away, on which he could never walk again. It was even more ironic that, through the most stupid accident of his life, he was still in excellent health when virtually all his old friends were dead.

He had been back on Earth only a week when, despite all the warnings and his own determination that nothing of the sort would ever happen to *him*, he had stepped off that second-story balcony. (Yes, he had been celebrating: but he had earned it—he was a hero on the new world to which *Leonov* had returned.) The multiple fractures had led to complications, which could best be handled in the Pasteur Space Hospital.

That had been 2015. And now—he could not really believe it, but there was the calendar on the wall—it was 2061.

For Heywood Floyd, the biological clock had not merely been slowed down by the one-sixth Earth-gravity of the hospital; twice in his life it had actually been reversed. It was now generally believed—though some authorities disputed it—that hibernation did more than merely stop the aging process; it encouraged rejuvenation. Floyd had actually become younger on his voyage to Jupiter and back.

"So you really think it's safe for me to go?"

"Nothing in this universe is *safe*, Heywood. All I can say is that there are no physiological objections. After all, your environment will be virtually the same aboard *Universe* as it is here. She may not have quite the standard of—ah—superlative medical expertise we can provide at Pasteur, but Dr. Mahindran is a good man. If there's any problem he can't cope with, he can put you into hibernation again and ship you back to us, C.O.D."

It was the verdict that Floyd had hoped for, yet somehow his pleasure was alloyed with sadness. He would be away for weeks from his home of almost half a century and the new friends of his later years. And although *Universe* was a luxury liner compared with the primitive *Leonov* (now hovering high above Farside as one of the main exhibits at the Lagrange Museum), there was still some element of risk in any extended space voyage. Especially like the pioneering one on which he was now preparing to embark . . .

Yet that, perhaps, was exactly what he was seeking—even at 103 (or, according to the complex geriatric accounting of the late Professor Katerina Rudenko, a hale and hearty 65). During the last decade, he had become aware of an increasing restlessness and a vague dissatisfaction with a life that was too comfortable and well ordered.

Despite all the exciting projects in progress around the Solar System—the Mars Renewal, the establishment of the Mercury Base, the Greening of Ganymede—there had been no goal on which he could really focus his interests and his still-considerable energies. Two centuries ago, one of the first poets of the Scientific Era had summed up his feelings perfectly, speaking through the lips of Odysseus/Ulysses:

> Life piled on life
> Were all too little, and of one of me
> Little remains; but every hour is saved
> From that eternal silence, something more,
> A bringer of new things: and vile it were
> For some three suns to store and hoard myself,
> And this grey spirit yearning in desire
> To follow knowledge like a sinking star,
> Beyond the utmost bound of human thought.

"Three suns," indeed! It was more than forty: Ulysses would have been ashamed of him. But the next verse—which he knew so well—was even more appropriate:

It may be that the gulfs will wash us down:
It may be we shall touch the Happy Isles,
And see the great Achilles, whom we knew.
Though much is taken, much abides; and though
We are not now that strength which in old days
Moved earth and heaven; that which we are, we are;
One equal temper of heroic hearts,
Made weak by time and fate, but strong in will
To strive, to seek, to find, and not to yield.

"To seek, to find . . ." Well, now he knew what he was going to seek *and* to find—because he knew exactly where it would be. Short of some catastrophic accident, there was no way in which it could possibly elude him.

It was not a goal he had ever consciously had in mind, and even now he was not quite sure why it had become so suddenly dominant. He would have thought himself immune to the fever that was once again infecting mankind—for the second time in his life!—but perhaps he was mistaken. Or it could have been that the unexpected invitation to join the short list of distinguished guests aboard *Universe* had fired his imagination and awakened an enthusiasm he had not even known he possessed.

There was another possibility. After all these years, he could still remember what an anticlimax the 1985–86 encounter had been to the general public. Now was a chance—the last for him, and the first for humanity—to more than make up for any previous disappointment.

Back in the twentieth century, only flybys had been possible. This time, there would be an actual landing, as pioneering in its way as Armstrong and Aldrin's first steps on the Moon.

Dr. Heywood Floyd, veteran of the 2010–15 mission to Jupiter, let his imagination fly outward to the ghostly visitor once again returning from the deeps of space, gaining speed second by second as it prepared to round the Sun. And between the orbits of Earth and Venus the most famous of all comets would meet the still-uncompleted spaceliner *Universe* on its maiden flight.

The exact point of rendezvous was not yet settled, but *his* decision was already made.

"Halley—here I come . . ." whispered Heywood Floyd.

2 · First Sight

It is not true that one must leave Earth to appreciate the full splendor of the heavens. Not even in space is the starry sky more glorious than when viewed from a high mountain, on a perfectly clear night, far from any source of artificial illumination. Even though the stars appear brighter beyond the atmosphere, the eye cannot really appreciate the difference: and the overwhelming spectacle of half the celestial sphere at a single glance is something that no observation window can provide.

But Heywood Floyd was more than content with his private view of the universe, especially during the times when the residential zone was on the shadow side of the slowly revolving space hospital. Then there would be nothing in his rectangular field of view but stars, planets, nebulae—and occasionally, drowning out all else, the unblinking glare of Lucifer, new rival to the Sun.

About ten minutes before the beginning of his artificial night, he would switch off all the cabin lights—even the red emergency standby—so that he could become completely dark-adapted. A little late in life for a space engineer, he had learned the pleasures of naked-eye astronomy, and could now identify virtually any constellation, even if he could glimpse only a small portion of it.

Almost every "night" that May, as the comet was passing inside the orbit of Mars, he had checked its location on the star charts. Although it was an easy object to find with a good pair of binoculars, Floyd had stubbornly resisted their aid; he was playing a little game, seeing how well his aging eyes would respond to the challenge. Though two astronomers on Mauna Kea already claimed to have observed the comet visually, no one believed them, and similar assertions from other residents of Pasteur had been treated with even greater skepticism.

But tonight, a magnitude of at least six was predicted; he might be in luck. He traced the line from Gamma to Epsilon, and stared toward the apex of an imaginary equilateral triangle set upon it—almost as if he could focus his vision across the Solar System by a sheer effort of will.

And there it was!—just as he had first seen it, seventy-six years ago, inconspicuous but unmistakable. If he had not known exactly where to look, he would not even have noticed it, or would have dismissed it as some distant nebula.

To his naked eye it was merely a tiny, perfectly circular blob of mist; strain as he could, he was unable to detect any trace of a tail. But the small flotilla of probes that had been escorting the comet for months had already recorded the first outbursts of dust and gas that would soon create a glowing plume across the stars, pointing directly away from its creator, the Sun.

Like everyone else, Heywood Floyd had watched the transformation of the cold, dark—no, almost *black*—nucleus as it entered the inner Solar System. After seventy years of deep freeze, the complex mixture of water, ammonia, and other ices was beginning to thaw and bubble. A flying mountain roughly the shape—and size—of the island of Manhattan was turning on a cosmic spit every fifty-three hours; as the heat of the Sun seeped through the insulating crust, the vaporizing gases were making Halley's Comet behave like a leaking steam boiler. Jets of water vapor, mixed with dust and a witch's brew of organic chemicals, were bursting out from half a dozen small craters; the largest—about the size of a football field—erupted regularly about two hours after local dawn. It looked exactly like a terrestrial geyser, and had been promptly christened "Old Faithful."

Already, he had fantasies of standing on the rim of that crater, waiting for the Sun to rise above the dark, contorted landscape that he already knew well through the images from space. True, the contract said nothing about passengers—as opposed to crew and scientific personnel—going outside the ship when it landed on Halley.

On the other hand, there was also nothing in the small print that specifically forbade it.

They'll have a job to stop me, thought Heywood Floyd; I'm sure I can still handle a spacesuit. And if I'm wrong—

He remembered reading that a visitor to the Taj Mahal had once remarked: "I'd die tomorrow for a monument like this."

He would gladly settle for Halley's comet.

3 · Reentry

Even apart from that embarrassing accident, the return to Earth had not been easy.

The first shock had come soon after revival, when Dr. Rudenko had awakened him from his long sleep. Walter Curnow was hovering beside her, and even in his semiconscious state Floyd could tell that something was wrong; their pleasure at seeing him awake was a little too exaggerated, and failed to conceal a sense of strain. Not until he was fully recovered did they let him know that Dr. Chandra was no longer with them.

Somewhere beyond Mars, so imperceptibly that the monitors could not pinpoint the time, he had simply ceased to live. His body, set adrift in space, had continued unchecked along *Leonov*'s orbit and had long since been consumed by the fires of the sun.

The cause of death was totally unknown, but Max Brailovsky expressed a view that, highly unscientific though it was, not even Surgeon-Commander Katerina Rudenko attempted to refute.

"He couldn't live without Hal."

Walter Curnow, of all people, added another thought.

"I wonder how Hal will take it. Something out there must be monitoring all our broadcasts. Sooner or later, he'll know."

And now Curnow was gone too—so were they all except little Zenia. He had not seen her for twenty years, but her card arrived punctually every Christmas. The last one was still pinned above his desk; it showed a troika laden with gifts speeding through the snows of a Russian winter, watched by extremely hungry-looking wolves.

Forty-five years! Sometimes it seemed only yesterday that *Leonov* had returned to Earth orbit and the applause of all mankind. Yet it had been a curiously subdued applause, respectful but lacking genuine enthusiasm. The mission to Jupiter had been altogether too much of a success; it had opened a Pandora's box, the full contents of which had yet to be disclosed.

When the black monolith known as Tycho Magnetic Anomaly One had been excavated on the Moon, only a handful of men knew of its existence. Not until after *Discovery*'s ill-fated voyage to Jupiter did the world learn that, four million years ago, another intelligence had passed through the Solar System and left its calling card. The news was a revelation—but not a surprise; something of the sort had been expected for decades.

And it had all happened long before the human race existed. Although some mysterious accident had befallen *Discovery* out around Jupiter, there was no real evidence that it involved anything more than a shipboard malfunction. Although the philosophical consequences of TMA-1 were profound, for all practical purposes Mankind was still alone in the Universe.

Now that was no longer true. Only light-minutes away—a mere stone's throw in the Cosmos—was an intelligence that could create a star and, for its own inscrutable purpose, destroy a planet a thousand times the size of Earth. Even more ominous was the fact that it had shown awareness of Mankind, through the last message that *Discovery* had beamed back from the moons of Jupiter just before the fiery birth of Lucifer had destroyed it:

ALL THESE WORLDS ARE YOURS—EXCEPT EUROPA.
ATTEMPT NO LANDINGS THERE.

The brilliant new star, which had banished night except for the few months in each year when it was passing behind the Sun, had brought both hope and fear to Mankind. Fear—because the unknown, especially when it appeared linked with omnipotence, could not fail to rouse such primeval emotions. Hope—because of the transformation it had wrought in global politics.

It had often been said that the only thing that could unite Mankind was a threat from space. Whether Lucifer was a threat, no one knew; but it was certainly a challenge. And that, as it turned out, was enough.

Heywood Floyd had watched the geopolitical changes from his vantage point on Pasteur, almost as if he were an alien observer himself. At first, he had no intention of remaining in space, once his recovery was complete. To the baffled annoyance of his doctors, that took an altogether unreasonable length of time.

Looking back from the tranquillity of later years, Floyd knew exactly why his bones refused to mend. He simply did not wish to return to Earth: there was nothing for him down on the dazzling blue-and-white globe that filled his sky. There were times when he could well understand how Chandra might have lost the will to live.

It was pure chance that he had not been with his first wife on that flight to Europe. Now Marion was dead, her memory seemed part of another life that might have belonged to someone else, and their two daughters were amiable strangers with families of their own.

But he had lost Caroline through his own actions, even though he had no real choice in the matter. She had never understood (had he really done so himself?) why he had left the beautiful home they had made together to exile himself for years in the cold wastes far from the Sun.

Though he had known, even before the mission was half over, that Caroline would not wait, he had hoped desperately that Chris would forgive him. But even this consolation had been denied; his son had been without a father for too long. By the time Floyd returned, Chris had found another in the man who had taken Floyd's place in Caroline's life. The estrangement was complete; Floyd thought he would never get over it, but of course he did—after a fashion.

His body had cunningly conspired with his unconscious desires. When at last he returned to Earth after his protracted convalescence in Pasteur, he promptly developed such alarming symptoms—including something suspiciously like bone necrosis—that he was immediately rushed back to orbit. And there he had stayed, apart from a few excursions to the Moon, completely adapted to living in the zero to one-sixth gravity regime of the slowly rotating space hospital.

He was not a recluse—far from it. Even while he was convalescing, he was dictating reports, giving evidence to endless commissions, being interviewed by media representatives. He was a famous man and enjoyed the experience—while it lasted. It helped to compensate for his inner wounds.

The first complete decade—2020 to 2030—seemed to have passed so swiftly that he now found it difficult to focus upon it. There were the usual crises, scandals, crimes, catastrophes—notably the Great Californian Earthquake, whose aftermath he had watched with fascinated horror through the station's monitor screens. Under their greatest magnification, in favorable conditions, they could show individual human beings; but from his God's-eye-view it had been impossible to identify with the scurrying dots fleeing from the burning cities. Only the ground cameras revealed the true horror.

During that decade, though the results would not be apparent until later, the political tectonic plates were moving as inexorably as the geological ones—yet in the opposite sense, as if Time were running backward. For in the beginning, the Earth had possessed the single supercontinent of Pangea, which over the eons had split asunder. So had the human species, into innumerable tribes and nations; now it was merging together, as the old linguistic and cultural divisions began to blur.

Although Lucifer had accelerated the process, it had begun decades earlier, when the coming of the jet age had triggered an explosion of global tourism. At almost the same time—it was not, of course, a coincidence—satellites and fiber optics had revolutionized communications. With the historic abolition of long-distance charges on 31 December 2000, every telephone call became a local one, and the human race greeted the new millennium by transforming itself into one huge, gossiping family.

Like most families, it was not always a peaceful one, but its disputes no longer threatened the entire planet. The second—and last—nuclear war saw the use in combat of no more bombs than the first: precisely two. And though the kilotonnage was greater, the casualties were far fewer, as both were used against sparsely populated oil installations. At that point the Big Three of China, the US, and the USSR moved with commendable speed and wisdom, sealing off the battle zone until the surviving combatants had come to their senses.

By the decade of 2020–30, a major war between Great Powers was as unthinkable as one between Canada and the United States had been in the century before. This was not due to any vast improvement in human nature, or indeed to any single factor except the normal preference for life over death. Much of the machinery of peace was not even consciously planned: before the politicians realized what had happened, they discovered that it was in place, and functioning well . . .

No statesman, no idealist of any persuasion invented the "Peace Hostage" movement; the very name was not coined until well after someone had noticed that at any given moment there were a hundred thousand Russian tourists in the United States—and half a million Americans in the Soviet Union, most of them engaged in their traditional pastime of complaining about the plumbing. And perhaps even more to the point, both groups contained a disproportionately large number of highly nonexpendable individuals—the sons and daughters of wealth, privilege, and political power.

And even if one wished, it was no longer possible to plan a large-scale war. The Age of Transparency had dawned in the 1990s, when enterprising news media had started to launch photographic satellites with resolutions comparable to those that the military had possessed for three decades. The Pentagon and the Kremlin were furious; but they were no match for Reuters, Associated Press, and the unsleeping, twenty-four-hours-a-day cameras of the Orbital News Service.

By 2060, even though the world had not been completely disarmed, it had been effectively pacified, and the fifty remaining nuclear weapons were all under international control. There was surprisingly little opposition

when that popular monarch, Edward VIII, was elected the first Planetary
President, only a dozen states dissenting. They ranged in size and importance from the still-stubbornly neutral Swiss (whose restaurants and hotels
nevertheless greeted the new bureaucracy with open arms) to the even
more fanatically independent Malvinians, who now resisted all attempts by
the exasperated British and Argentines to foist them off on each other.

The dismantling of the vast and wholly parasitic armaments industry
had given an unprecedented—sometimes, indeed, unhealthy—boost to the
world economy. No longer were vital raw materials and brilliant engineering talents swallowed up in a virtual black hole—or, even worse, turned to
destruction. Instead, they could be used to repair the ravages and neglect
of centuries, by rebuilding the world.

And building new ones. Now indeed Mankind had found the "moral
equivalent of War," and a challenge that could absorb the surplus energies
of the race—for as many millennia ahead as anyone dared to dream.

4 · Tycoon

When he was born, William Tsung had been called "the most expensive baby in the world"; he held the title for only two years before it was claimed by his sister. She still held it, and now that the Family Laws had been repealed, it would never be challenged.

Their father, the legendary Sir Lawrence, had been born when China had reinstituted the stringent "One Child, One Family" rule; his generation had provided psychologists and social scientists with material for endless studies. Having no brothers or sisters—and in many cases, no uncles or aunts—it was unique in human history. Whether credit was due to the resilience of the species or the merit of the Chinese extended family system would probably never be settled. The fact remained that the children of that strange time were remarkably free from scars; but they were certainly not unaffected, and Sir Lawrence had done his somewhat spectacular best to make up for the isolation of his infancy.

When his second child was born in '22, the licensing system had become law. You could have as many children as you wished, provided only that you paid the appropriate fee. (The surviving Old Guard communists were not the only ones who thought the whole scheme perfectly appalling, but they were outvoted by their pragmatic colleagues in the fledgling congress of the People's Democratic Republic.)

Numbers 1 and 2 were free. Number 3 cost a million sols. Number 4 was two million. Number 5 was four million, and so on. The fact that, in theory, there were no capitalists in the People's Republic was cheerfully ignored.

Young Mr. Tsung (that was years, of course, before King Edward made

him a Knight Commander of the Order of the British Empire) never revealed if he had any target in mind; he was still a fairly poor millionaire
when his fifth child was born. But he was still only forty, and when the
purchase of Hong Kong did not take quite as much of his capital as he had
feared, he discovered that he had a considerable amount of small change in
hand.

So ran the legend—but, like many other stories about Sir Lawrence, it
was hard to distinguish fact from mythology. There was certainly no truth
in the persistent rumor that he had made his first fortune through the
famous shoebox-sized pirate edition of the Library of Congress. The whole
Molecular Memory Module racket was an off-Earth operation, made possible by the United States' failure to sign the Lunar Treaty.

Even though Sir Lawrence was not a multitrillionaire, the complex of
corporations he had built up made him the greatest financial power on
Earth—no small achievement for the son of a humble video-cassette ped-
dler in what was still known as the New Territories. He probably never
noticed the eight million for child Number Six, or even the thirty-two for
Number Eight. The sixty-four he had to advance on Number Nine attracted world publicity, and after Number Ten the bets placed on his
future plans may well have exceeded the two hundred and fifty-six million
the next child would have cost him. However, at that point the Lady
Jasmine, who combined the best properties of steel and silk in exquisite
proportion, decided that the Tsung dynasty was adequately established.

It was quite by chance (if there is such a thing) that Sir Lawrence
became personally involved in the space business. He had, of course, extensive maritime and aeronautical interests, but these were handled by his five
sons and their associates. Sir Lawrence's real love was communications—
newspapers (those few that were left), books, magazines (paper and electronic), and, above all, the global television networks.

Then he had bought the magnificent old Peninsular Hotel, which to a
poor Chinese boy had once seemed the very symbol of wealth and power,
and turned it into his residence and main office. He surrounded it by a
beautiful park, by the simple expedient of pushing the huge shopping centers underground (his newly formed Laser Excavation Corporation made a
fortune in the process and set a precedent for many other cities.)

One day, as he was admiring the unparalleled skyline of the city across
the harbor, he decided that a further improvement was necessary. The
view from the lower floors of the Peninsular had been blocked for decades
by a large building looking like a squashed golfball. This, Sir Lawrence
decided, would have to go.

The director of the Hong Kong Planetarium—widely considered to be
among the five best in the world—had other ideas, and very soon Sir

Lawrence was delighted to discover someone he could not buy at any price. The two men became firm friends; but when Dr. Hessenstein arranged a special presentation for Sir Lawrence's sixtieth birthday, he did not know that he would help to change the history of the Solar System.

5 · Out of the Ice

More than a hundred years after Zeiss had built the first prototype in Jena in 1924, there were still a few optical planetarium projectors in use, looming dramatically over their audiences. But Hong Kong had retired its third-generation instrument decades ago, in favor of the far more versatile electronic system. The whole of the great dome was, essentially, a giant television screen, made up of thousands of separate panels, on which any conceivable image could be displayed.

The program had opened—inevitably—with a tribute to the unknown inventor of the rocket, somewhere in China during the thirteenth century. The first five minutes were a high-speed historical survey, giving perhaps less than due credit to the Russian, German, and American pioneers in order to concentrate on the career of Dr. Hsue-Shen Tsien. His countrymen could be excused, in such a time and place, if they made him appear as important in the history of rocket development as Goddard, von Braun, or Korolyev. And they certainly had just grounds for indignation at his arrest on trumped-up charges in the United States when, after helping to establish the famed Jet Propulsion Laboratory and being appointed CalTech's first Goddard Professor, he decided to return to his homeland.

The launching of the first Chinese satellite by the Long March 1 rocket in 1970 was barely mentioned, perhaps because at that time the Americans were already walking on the Moon. Indeed, the rest of the twentieth century was dismissed in a few minutes, to take the story up to 2007 and the secret construction of the spaceship *Tsien*—in full view of the whole world.

The narrator did not gloat unduly over the consternation of the other spacefaring powers when a presumed Chinese space station suddenly blasted out of orbit and headed for Jupiter, to overtake the Russian-American mission aboard the *Cosmonaut Alexei Leonov*. The story was dramatic —and tragic—enough to require no embellishment.

Unfortunately, there was very little authentic visual material to illustrate it: the program had to rely largely on special effects and intelligent reconstruction from later, long-range photosurveys. During their brief sojourn on the icy surface of Europa, *Tsien*'s crew had been far too busy to make television documentaries or even set up an unattended camera.

Nevertheless, the words spoken at the time conveyed much of the drama of that first landing on the moons of Jupiter. The commentary broadcast from the approaching *Leonov* by Heywood Floyd served admirably to set the scene, and there were plenty of library shots of Europa to illustrate it:

"At this very moment I'm looking at it through the most powerful of the ship's telescopes: under this magnification, it's ten times larger than the Moon as you see it with naked eye. And it's a really *weird* sight.

"The surface is a uniform pink, with a few small brown patches. It's covered with an intricate network of narrow lines, curling and weaving in all directions. In fact, it looks very much like a photo from a medical textbook, showing a pattern of veins and arteries.

"A few of these features are hundreds—or even thousands—of kilometers long, and look rather like the illusory canals that Percival Lowell and other early-twentieth-century astronomers imagined they'd seen on Mars.

"But Europa's canals aren't an illusion, though of course they're not artificial. What's more, they *do* contain water—or at least ice. For the satellite is almost entirely covered by ocean, averaging fifty kilometers deep.

"Because it's so far from the Sun, Europa's surface temperature is extremely low—about a hundred and fifty degrees below freezing. So one might expect its single ocean to be a solid block of ice.

"Surprisingly, that isn't the case because there's a lot of heat generated inside Europa by tidal forces—the same forces that drive the great volcanoes on neighboring Io.

"So the ice is continually melting, breaking up, and freezing, forming cracks and lanes like those in the floating ice sheets in our own polar regions. It's that intricate tracery of cracks I'm seeing now; most of them are dark and very ancient—perhaps millions of years old. But a few are almost pure white; they're the new ones that have just opened up, and have a crust only a few centimeters thick.

"*Tsien* has landed right beside one of these white streaks—the fifteen-hundred-kilometer-long feature that's been christened the Grand Canal. Presumably the Chinese intend to pump its water into their propellant tanks, so that they can explore the Jovian satellite system and then return to Earth. That may not be easy, but they'll certainly have studied the landing site with great care, and must know what they're doing.

"It's obvious, now, why they've taken such a risk—and why they claim Europa. As a refueling point. It could be the key to the entire Solar System . . ."

But it hadn't worked out that way, thought Sir Lawrence, as he reclined in his luxurious chair beneath the streaked and mottled disk that filled his artificial sky. The oceans of Europa were still inaccessible to Mankind, for reasons that were still a mystery. And not only inaccessible, but invisible; since Jupiter had become a sun, both its inner satellites had vanished beneath clouds of vapor boiling out from their interiors. He was looking at Europa as it had been back in 2010—not as it was today.

He had been little more than a boy then, but could still remember the pride he felt in knowing that his countrymen—however much he disapproved of their politics—were about to make the first landing on a virgin world.

There had been no camera there, of course, to record that landing, but the reconstruction was superbly done. He could really believe that was the doomed spaceship dropping silently out of the jet-black sky toward the Europan icescape and coming to rest beside the discolored band of recently frozen water that had been christened the Grand Canal.

Everyone knew what had happened next; perhaps wisely, there had been no attempt to reproduce it visually. Instead, the image of Europa faded, to be replaced by a portrait as familiar to every Chinese as Yuri Gagarin's was to every Russian.

The first photograph showed Rupert Chang on his graduation day in 1989—the earnest young scholar, indistinguishable from a million others, utterly unaware of his appointment with history two decades in the future.

Briefly, to a background of subdued music, the commentator summed up the highlights of Dr. Chang's career, until his appointment as Science Officer aboard *Tsien*. Cross-sections in time, the photographs grew older until the last one, taken immediately before the mission.

Sir Lawrence was glad of the planetarium's darkness; both his friends and his enemies would have been surprised to see the moisture gathering in his eyes as he listened to the message that Dr. Chang had aimed toward the approaching *Leonov*, never knowing if it would be received:

". . . know you are aboard *Leonov* . . . may not have much time . . . aiming my suit antenna where I think . . ."

The signal vanished for agonizing seconds, then came back much clearer, though not appreciably louder.

". . . relay this information to Earth. *Tsien* destroyed three hours ago. I'm only survivor. Using my suit radio—no idea if it has enough range, but

it's the only chance. Please listen carefully. THERE IS LIFE ON EU-
ROPA. I repeat: THERE IS LIFE ON EUROPA . . . ."

The signal faded again . . .

" . . . soon after local midnight. We were pumping steadily and the
tanks were almost half full. Dr. Lee and I went out to check the pipe
insulation. *Tsien* stands—stood—about thirty meters from the edge of the
Grand Canal. Pipes go directly from it and down through the ice. Very
thin—not safe to walk on. The warm upwelling . . ."

Again a long silence . . .

" . . . no problem—five kilowatts of lighting strung up on the ship. Like
a Christmas tree—beautiful, shining right through the ice. Glorious colors.
Lee saw it first—a huge dark mass rising up from the depths. At first we
thought it was a school of fish—too large for a single organism—then it
started to break through the ice . . .

" . . . like huge strands of wet seaweed, crawling along the ground. Lee
ran back to the ship to get a camera—I stayed to watch, reporting over the
radio. The thing moved so slowly I could easily outrun it. I was much
more excited than alarmed. Thought I knew what kind of creature it was
—I've seen pictures of the kelp forests off California—but I was quite
wrong.

" . . . I could tell it was in trouble. It couldn't possibly survive at a
temperature a hundred and fifty below its normal environment. It was
freezing solid as it moved forward—bits were breaking off like glass—but
it was still advancing toward the ship, a black tidal wave, slowing down all
the time.

"I was still so surprised that I couldn't think straight and I couldn't
imagine what it was trying to do . . ."

" . . . climbing up the ship, building a kind of ice tunnel as it advanced.
Perhaps this was insulating it from the cold—the way termites protect
themselves from sunlight with their little corridors of mud.

" . . . tons of ice on the ship. The radio antennas broke off first. Then I
could see the landing legs beginning to buckle—all in slow motion, like a
dream.

"Not until the ship started to topple did I realize what the thing was
trying to do—and then it was too late. We could have saved ourselves—if
we'd only switched off those lights.

"Perhaps it's a phototrope, its biological cycle triggered by the sunlight
that filters through the ice. Or it could have been attracted like a moth to a
candle. Our floodlights must have been more brilliant than anything that
Europa has ever known . . .

"Then the ship crashed. I saw the hull split, a cloud of snowflakes form
as moisture condensed. All the lights went out, except for one, swinging
back and forth on a cable a couple of meters above the ground.

"I don't know what happened immediately after that. The next thing I remember, I was standing under the light, beside the wreck of the ship, with a fine powdering of fresh snow all around me. I could see my footsteps in it very clearly. I must have run there; perhaps only a minute or two had elapsed . . .

"The plant—I still thought of it as a plant—was motionless.
I wondered if it had been damaged by the impact; large sections—as thick as a man's arm—had splintered off, like broken twigs.

"Then the main trunk started to move again. It pulled away from the hull, and began to crawl toward me. That was when I knew for certain that the thing was light-sensitive: I was standing immediately under the thousand-watt lamp, which had stopped swinging now.

"Imagine an oak tree—better still, a banyan with its multiple trunks and roots—flattened out by gravity and trying to creep along the ground. It got to within five meters of the light, then started to spread out until it had made a perfect circle around me. Presumably that was the limit of its tolerance—the point at which photoattraction turned to repulsion. After that, nothing happened for several minutes. I wondered if it was dead—frozen solid at last.

"Then I saw that large buds were forming on many of the branches. It was like watching a time-lapse film of flowers opening. In fact I thought they *were* flowers—each about as big as a man's head.

"Delicate, beautifully colored membranes started to unfold. Even then, it occurred to me that no one—no *thing*—could ever have seen these colors before; they had no existence until we brought our lights—our fatal lights—to this world.

"Tendrils, stamens, waving feebly . . . I walked over to the living wall that surrounded me, so that I could see exactly what was happening. Neither then, or at any other time, had I felt the slightest fear of the creature. I was certain that it was not malevolent—if indeed it was conscious at all.

"There were scores of the big flowers, in various stages of unfolding. Now they reminded me of butterflies, just emerging from the chrysalis—wings crumpled, still feeble—I was getting closer and closer to the truth.

"But they were freezing—dying as quickly as they formed. Then, one after another, they dropped off from the parent buds. For a few moments they flopped around like fish stranded on dry land—and at last I realized exactly what they were. Those membranes weren't petals—they were *fins,* or their equivalent. This was the free-swimming, larval stage of the creature. Probably it spends much of its life rooted on the seabed, then sends these mobile offspring in search of new territory. Just like the corals of Earth's oceans.

"I knelt down to get a closer look at one of the little creatures. The beautiful colors were fading now, to a drab brown. Some of the petal-fins had snapped off, becoming brittle shards as they froze. But it was still moving feebly, and as I approached it tried to avoid me. I wondered how it sensed my presence.

"Then I noticed that the *stamens*—as I'd called them—all carried bright blue dots at their tips. They looked like tiny star sapphires—or the blue eyes along the mantle of a scallop—aware of light, but unable to form true images. As I watched, the vivid blue faded, the sapphires became dull, ordinary stones . . .

"Dr. Floyd—or anyone else who is listening—I haven't much more time; Jupiter will soon block my signal. But I've almost finished.

"I knew then what I had to do. The cable to that thousand-watt lamp was hanging almost to the ground. I gave it a few tugs, and the light went out in a shower of sparks.

"I wondered if it was too late. For a few minutes, nothing happened. So I walked over to the wall of tangled branches around me, and *kicked* it.

"Slowly, the creature started to unweave itself, and to retreat back to the Canal. There was plenty of light—I could see everything perfectly. Ganymede and Callisto were in the sky—Jupiter was a huge, thin crescent—and there was a big auroral display on the nightside, at the Jovian end of the Io flux tube. There was no need to use my helmet light.

"I followed the creature all the way back to the water, encouraging it with more kicks when it slowed down, feeling the fragments of ice crunching all the time beneath my boots . . . As it neared the canal, it seemed to gain strength and energy, as if it knew that it was approaching its natural home. I wondered if it would survive, to bud again.

"It disappeared through the surface, leaving a few last dead larvae on the alien land. The exposed free water bubbled for a few minutes until a scab of protective ice sealed it from the vacuum above. Then I walked back to the ship to see if there was anything to salvage—I don't want to talk about that.

"I've only two requests to make, Doctor. When the taxonomists classify this creature, I hope they'll name it after me.

"And—when the next ship comes home—ask them to take our bones back to China.

"Jupiter will be cutting us off in a few minutes. I wish I knew whether anyone was receiving me. Anyway, I'll repeat this message when we're in line of sight again—if my suit's life-support system lasts that long.

"This is Professor Chang on Europa, reporting the destruction of spaceship *Tsien*. We landed beside the Grand Canal and set up our pumps at the edge of the ice—"

The signal faded abruptly, came back for a moment, then disappeared completely below the noise level. There would never be any further message from Professor Chang; but it had already deflected Lawrence Tsung's ambitions into space.

6 · The Greening of Ganymede

Rolf van der Berg was the right man, in the right place, at the right time; no other combination would have worked. Which, of course, is how much of history is made.

He was the right man because he was a second-generation Afrikaner refugee and a trained geologist; both factors were equally important. He was in the right place, because that had to be the largest of the Jovian moons—third outward in the sequence Io, Europa, Ganymede, Callisto.

The time was not so critical, for the information had been ticking away like a delayed-action bomb in the data banks for at least a decade. van der Berg did not encounter it until '57; even then it took him another year to convince himself that he was not crazy—and it was '59 before he had quietly sequestered the original records so that no one could duplicate his discovery. Only then could he safely give his full attention to the main problem: what to do next.

It had all begun, as is so often the case, with an apparently trivial observation in a field that did not even concern van der Berg directly. His job, as a member of the Planetary Engineering Task Force, was to survey and catalog the natural resources of Ganymede; he had little business fooling around with the forbidden satellite next door.

But Europa was an enigma that no one—least of all its immediate neighbors—could ignore for long. Every seven days it passed between Ganymede and the brilliant minisun that had once been Jupiter, producing eclipses which could last as long as twelve minutes. At its closest, it appeared slightly smaller than the Moon as seen from Earth, but it dwindled to a mere quarter of that size when it was on the other side of its orbit.

The eclipses were often spectacular. Just before it slid between Ganymede and Lucifer, Europa would become an ominous black disk outlined with a ring of crimson fire as the light of the new sun was refracted through the atmosphere it had helped to create.

In less than half a human lifetime, Europa had been transformed. The crust of ice on the hemisphere always facing Lucifer had melted to form the Solar System's second ocean. For a decade it had foamed and bubbled into the vacuum above it, until equilibrium had been reached. Now Europa possessed a thin but serviceable—though not to human beings—atmosphere of water vapor, hydrogen sulfide, carbon and sulfur dioxides, nitrogen, and miscellaneous rare gases. Though the somewhat misnamed Nightside of the satellite was still permanently frozen, an area as large as Africa now had a temperate climate, liquid water, and a few scattered islands.

All this, and not much more, had been observed through telescopes in Earth orbit. By the time that the first full-scale expedition had been launched to the Galilean moons, in 2028, Europa had already become veiled by a permanent mantle of clouds. Cautious radar probing revealed little but smooth ocean on one face and almost equally smooth ice on the other; Europa still maintained its reputation as the flattest piece of real estate in the Solar System.

Ten years later, that was no longer true: something drastic had happened to Europa. It now possessed a solitary mountain, almost as high as Everest, jutting up through the ice of the twilight zone. Presumably some volcanic activity—like that occurring ceaselessly on neighboring Io—had thrust this mass of material skyward. The vastly increased heat-flow from Lucifer could have triggered such an event.

But there were problems with this obvious explanation. Mount Zeus was an irregular pyramid, not the usual volcanic cone, and radar scans showed none of the characteristic lava flows. Some poor-quality photographs obtained through telescopes on Ganymede, during a momentary break in the clouds, suggested that it was made of ice, like the frozen landscape around it. Whatever the answer, the creation of Mount Zeus had been a traumatic experience for the world it dominated, for the entire crazy-paving pattern of fractured ice floes over Nightside had changed completely.

One maverick scientist had put forward the theory that Mount Zeus was a "cosmic iceberg"—a cometary fragment that had dropped upon Europa from space; battered Callisto gave ample proof that such bombardments had occurred in the remote past. The theory was very unpopular on Ganymede, whose would-be colonists already had sufficient problems. They had been much relieved when van der Berg had refuted the theory convincingly; any mass of ice that size would have shattered on impact—and even if it hadn't, Europa's gravity, modest though it was, would have quickly brought about its collapse. Radar measurements showed that though Mount Zeus was indeed steadily sinking, its overall shape remained completely unaltered. Ice was not the answer.

The problem could, of course, have been settled by sending a single probe through the clouds of Europa. Unfortunately, whatever was beneath that almost permanent overcast did not encourage curiosity.

ALL THESE WORLDS ARE YOURS—EXCEPT EUROPA. ATTEMPT NO LANDINGS THERE.

That last message relayed from the spaceship *Discovery* just before its destruction had not been forgotten, but there had been endless arguments about its interpretation. Did "landings" refer to robot probes, or only to manned vehicles? And what about close flybys—manned or unmanned? Or balloons floating in the upper atmosphere?

The scientists were anxious to find out, but the general public was distinctly nervous. Any power that could detonate the mightiest planet in the Solar System was not to be trifled with. And it would take centuries to explore and exploit Io, Ganymede, Callisto, and the dozens of minor satellites; Europa could wait.

More than once, therefore, van der Berg had been told not to waste his valuable time on research of no practical importance, when there was so much to be done on Ganymede. ("Where can we find carbon—phosphorus —nitrates for the hydroponic farms? How stable is the Barnard Escarpment? Is there any danger of more mudslides in Phrygia?" And so on and so forth . . .) But he had inherited his Boer ancestors' well-deserved reputation for stubbornness; even when he was working on his numerous other projects, he kept looking over his shoulder at Europa.

And one day, just for a few hours, a gale from Nightside cleared the skies about Mount Zeus.

7 · Transit

"I too take leave of all I ever had . . ."

From what depths of memory had *that* line come swimming up to the surface? Heywood Floyd closed his eyes and tried to focus on to the past. It was certainly from a poem—and he had hardly read a line of poetry since leaving college. And little enough then, except during a short English Appreciation Seminar.

With no further clues, it might take the station Computer quite a while —perhaps as much as ten minutes—to locate the line in the whole body of English literature. But that would be cheating (not to mention expensive), and Floyd preferred to accept the intellectual challenge.

A war poem, of course—but which war? There had been so many in the twentieth century . . .

He was still searching through the mental mists when his guests arrived, moving with the effortless, slow-motion grace of longtime one-sixth-gravity residents. The society of Pasteur was strongly influenced by what had been christened "centrifugal stratification"; some people never left the zero gee of the Hub, while those who hoped one day to return to Earth preferred the almost-normal-weight regime out on the rim of the huge, slowly revolving disk.

George and Jerry were now Floyd's oldest and closest friends—which was suprising, because they had so few obvious points in common. Looking back on his own somewhat checkered emotional career—two marriages, three formal contracts, two informal ones, three children—he often envied the long-term stability of their relationship, apparently quite unaffected by the "nephews" from Earth or Moon who visited them from time to time.

"Haven't you *ever* thought of divorce?" he had once asked them teasingly.

As usual, George—whose acrobatic yet profoundly serious conducting had been largely responsible for the comeback of the classical orchestra—was at no loss for words.

"Divorce—never," was his swift reply. "Murder—*often.*"

"Of course, he'd never get away with it," Jerry had retorted. "Sebastian would spill the beans."

Sebastian was a beautiful and talkative parrot that the couple had imported after a long battle with the hospital authorities. He could not only talk but could reproduce the opening bars of the Sibelius violin concerto, with which Jerry—considerably helped by Antonio Stradivari—had made his reputation half a century ago.

Now the time had come to say good-bye to George, Jerry, and Sebastian —perhaps only for a few weeks, perhaps forever. Floyd had already made all his other farewells, in a round of parties that had gravely depleted the station's wine cellar, and could think of nothing he had left undone.

Archie, his early-model but still perfectly serviceable comsec, had been programmed to handle all incoming messages, either by sending out appropriate replies or by routing anything urgent and personal to him aboard *Universe.* It would be strange, after all these years, not to be able to talk to anyone he wished—though in compensation he could also avoid unwanted callers. After a few days into the voyage, the ship would be far enough from Earth to make real-time conversation impossible, and all communication would have to be by recorded voice or teletext.

"We thought you were our friend," complained George. "It was a dirty trick to make us your executors—especially as you're not going to leave us anything."

"You may have a few surprises." Floyd grinned. "Anyway, Archie will take care of all the details. I'd just like you to monitor my mail, in case there's anything he doesn't understand."

"If *he* won't, neither will we. What do we know about all your scientific societies and that sort of nonsense?"

"They can look after themselves. Please see that the cleaning staff doesn't mess things up too badly while I'm away—and, if I don't come back—here are a few personal items I'd like delivered—mostly family."

Family! There were pains, as well as pleasures, in living as long as he had done.

It had been sixty-three—*sixty-three!*—years since Marion had died in that air crash. Now he felt a twinge of guilt, because he could not even recall the grief he must have known. Or at best, it was a synthetic reconstruction, not a genuine memory.

What would they have meant to each other, had she still been alive? She would have been just a hundred years old by now . . .

And now the two little girls he had once loved so much were friendly, gray-haired strangers in their late sixties, with children—and grandchildren!—of their own. At last count there had been nine on that side of the family; without Archie's help, he would never be able to keep track of their names. But at least they all remembered him at Christmas, through duty if not affection.

His second marriage, of course, had overlain the memories of his first, like the later writing on a medieval palimpsest. That too had ended, fifty years ago, somewhere between Earth and Jupiter. Though he had hoped for a reconciliation with both wife and son, there had been time for only one brief meeting, among all the welcoming ceremonies, before his accident exiled him to Pasteur.

The meeting had not been a success: nor had the second, arranged at considerable expense and difficulty aboard the space hospital itself—indeed, in this very room. Chris had been twenty then, and had just married; if there was one thing that united Floyd and Caroline, it was disapproval of his choice.

Yet Helena had turned out remarkably well: she had been a good mother to Chris II, born barely a month after the marriage. And when, like so many other young wives, she was widowed by the Copernicus Disaster, she did not lose her head.

There was a curious irony in the fact that both Chris I and II had lost their fathers to Space, though in very different ways. Floyd had returned briefly to his eight-year-old son as a total stranger; Chris II had at least known a father for the first decade of his life, before losing him forever.

And where *was* Chris these days? Neither Caroline nor Helena—who were now the best of friends—seemed to know whether he was on Earth or in space. But that was typical; only postcards date-stamped CLAVIUS BASE had informed his family of his first visit to the Moon.

Floyd's card was still taped prominently above his desk. Chris II had a good sense of humor—and of history. He had mailed his grandfather that famous photograph of the monolith looming over the spacesuited figures gathered round it in the Tycho excavation, more than half a century ago. All the others in the group were now dead, and the monolith itself was no longer on the Moon. In 2006, after much controversy, it had been brought to Earth and erected—an uncanny echo of the main building—in the United Nations Plaza. It had been intended to remind the human race that it was no longer alone; five years later, with Lucifer blazing in the sky, no such reminder was needed.

Floyd's fingers were not very steady—sometimes his right hand seemed to have a will of its own—as he unpeeled the card and slipped it into his pocket. It would be almost the only personal possession he would take when he boarded *Universe*.

"Twenty-five days—you'll be back before we've noticed you're gone," said Jerry. "And by the way, is it true that you'll have Dimitri onboard?"

"That little Cossack!" George snorted. "I conducted his Second Symphony, back in '22."

"Wasn't that when the First Violin threw up during the Largo?"

"No—that was Mahler, not Mihailovich. And anyway it was the brass, so nobody noticed—except the unlucky tuba player, who sold his instrument the next day."

"You're making this up!"

"Of course. But give the old rascal my love, and ask him if he remembers that night we had out in Vienna. Who else have you got aboard?"

"I've heard horrible rumors about press-gangs," said Jerry thoughtfully.

"Greatly exaggerated, I can assure you. We've all been personally chosen by Sir Lawrence for our intelligence, wit, beauty, charisma, or other redeeming virtue."

"Not expendability?"

"Well, now that you mention it, we've all had to sign a depressing legal document absolving Tsung Spacelines from every conceivable liability. My copy's in that file, by the way."

"Any chance of us collecting on it?" asked George hopefully.

"No—my lawyers say it's iron-clad. Tsung agrees to take me to Halley and back, give me food, water, air, and a room with a view."

"And in return?"

"When I get back I'll do my best to promote future voyages, make some video appearances, write a few articles—all very reasonable, for the chance of a lifetime. Oh yes—I'll also entertain my fellow passengers—and vice versa."

"How? Song and dance?"

"Well, I hope to inflict selected portions of my memoirs on a captive audience. But I don't think I'll be able to compete with the professionals. Did you know that Yva Merlin will be on board?"

"What! How did they coax her out of that Park Avenue cell?"

"She must be a hundred and—oops, sorry, Hey."

"She's seventy, plus or minus five."

"Forget the minus. I was just a kid when *Napoleon* came out."

There was a long pause while each of the trio scanned his memories of that famous work. Although some critics considered her Scarlett O'Hara to be her finest role, to the general public Yva Merlin (*née* Evelyn Miles, when she was born in Cardiff, South Wales) was still identified with Josephine. Almost half a century ago, David Griffin's controversial epic had delighted the French and infuriated the British—though both sides now agreed that he had occasionally allowed his artistic impulses to trifle with the historical record, notably in the spectacular final sequence of the emperor's coronation in Westminster Abbey.

"That's quite a scoop for Sir Lawrence," said George thoughtfully.

"I think I can claim some credit for that. Her father was an astronomer —he worked for me at one time—and she's always been quite interested in science. So I made a few video calls."

Heywood Floyd did not feel it necessary to add that, like a substantial fraction of the human race, he had fallen in love with Yva ever since the appearance of GWTW Mark II.

"Of course," he continued, "Sir Lawrence was delighted—but I had to convince him that she had more than a casual interest in astronomy. Otherwise the voyage could be a social disaster."

"Which reminds me," said George, producing a small package he had been not-very-successfully hiding behind his back. "We have a little present for you."

"Can I open it now?"

"Do you think he should?" Jerry wondered anxiously.

"In that case, I certainly will," said Floyd, untying the bright green ribbon and unwrapping the paper.

Inside was a nicely framed painting. Although Floyd knew little of art, he had seen it before; indeed, who could ever forget it?

The makeshift raft tossing on the waves was crowded with half-naked castaways, some already moribund, others waving desperately at a ship on the horizon. Beneath it was the caption:

THE RAFT OF THE MEDUSA
(Theodore Gericault, 1791–1824)

And underneath *that* was the message, signed by George and Jerry: "Getting there is half the fun."

"You're a pair of bastards, and I love you dearly," said Floyd, embracing them both. The ATTENTION light on Archie's keyboard was flashing briskly; it was time to go.

His friends left in a silence more eloquent than words. For the last time, Heywood Floyd looked around the little room that had been his universe for almost half his life.

And suddenly he remembered how that poem ended:

"I have been happy: happy now I go."

8 · Starfleet

Sir Lawrence Tsung was not a sentimental man and was far too cosmopolitan to take patriotism seriously—though as an undergraduate he had briefly sported one of the artificial pigtails worn during the Third Cultural Revolution. Yet the planetarium reenactment of the *Tsien* disaster moved him deeply, and caused him to focus much of his enormous influence and energy upon space.

Before long, he was taking weekend trips to the Moon, and had appointed his second-youngest son Charles (the thirty-two-million-sol one) as Vice-President of Tsung Astrofreight. The new corporation had only two catapult-launched, hydrogen-fueled ramrockets of less than a thousand tons empty mass; they would soon be obsolete, but they could provide Charles with the experience that, Sir Lawrence was quite certain, would be needed in the decades ahead. For at long last, the Space Age was truly about to begin.

Little more than half a century had separated the Wright Brothers and the coming of cheap, mass air transportation; it had taken twice as long to meet the far greater challenge of the Solar System.

Yet when Luis Alvarez and his team had discovered muon-catalyzed fusion back in the 1950s, it had seemed no more than a tantalizing laboratory curiosity, of only theoretical interest. Just as the great Lord Rutherford had pooh-poohed the prospects of atomic power, so Alvarez himself doubted that "cold nuclear fusion" would ever be of practical importance. Indeed, it was not until 2040 that the unexpected and accidental manufacture of stable muonium-hydrogen "compounds" had opened up a new chapter of human history—exactly as the discovery of the neutron had initiated the Atomic Age.

Now small, portable nuclear power plants could be built, with a minimum of shielding. Such enormous investments had already been made in conventional fusion that the world's electrical utilities were not—at first—affected, but the impact on space travel was immediate; it could be paralleled only by the jet revolution in air transport of a hundred years earlier.

No longer energy-limited, spacecraft could achieve far greater speeds; flight times in the Solar System could now be measured in weeks rather than months or even years. But the muon drive was still a reaction device—a sophisticated rocket, no different in principle from its chemically fueled ancestors; it needed a working fluid to give it thrust. And the cheapest, cleanest, and most convenient of all working fluids was—plain water.

The Pacific Spaceport was not likely to run short of this useful substance. Matters were different at the next port of call—the Moon. Not a trace of water had been discovered by the Surveyor, Apollo, and Luna missions. If the Moon had ever possessed any native water, eons of meteoric bombardment had boiled and blasted it into space.

Or so the selenologists believed: yet clues to the contrary had been visible ever since Galileo had turned his first telescope upon the Moon. Some lunar mountains, for a few hours after dawn, glitter as brilliantly as if they are capped with snow. The most famous case is the rim of the magnificent crater Aristarchus, which William Herschel, the father of modern astronomy, once observed shining so brightly in the lunar night that he decided it must be an active volcano. He was wrong; what he saw was the Earthlight reflected from a thin and transient layer of frost, condensed during the three hundred hours of freezing darkness.

The discovery of the great ice deposits beneath Schroter's Valley, the sinuous canyon winding away from Aristarchus, was the last factor in the equation that would transform the economics of space flight. The Moon could provide a filling station just where it was needed, high up on the outermost slopes of the Earth's gravitational field, at the beginning of the long haul to the planets.

Cosmos, first of the Tsung fleet, had been designed to carry freight and passengers on the Earth–Moon–Mars run—and as a test vehicle, through complex deals with a dozen organizations and governments, of the still-experimental muon drive. Built at the Imbrium shipyards, she had just sufficient thrust to lift off from the Moon with zero payload; operating from orbit to orbit, she would never again touch the surface of any world. With his usual flair for publicity, Sir Lawrence arranged for her maiden flight to commence on the hundredth anniversary of Sputnik Day, 4 October 2057.

Two years later, *Cosmos* was joined by a sister ship. *Galaxy* was designed for the Earth–Jupiter run, and had enough thrust to operate directly to any of the Jovian moons, though at considerable sacrifice of payload. If necessary, she could even return to her lunar berth for refitting. She was by far the swiftest vehicle ever built by man: if she burned up her entire propellant mass in one orgasm of acceleration, she would attain a speed of a thousand kilometers a second—which would take her from Earth to Jupiter in a week, and to the nearest star in not much more than ten thousand years.

The third ship of the fleet—and Sir Lawrence's pride and joy—embodied all that had been learned in the building of her two sisters. But *Universe* was not intended primarily for freight. She was designed from the beginning as the first passenger liner to cruise the space lanes—right out to Saturn, the jewel of the Solar System.

Sir Lawrence had planned something even more spectacular for her maiden voyage, but construction delays caused by a dispute with the Lunar Chapter of the Reformed Teamster's Union had upset his schedule. There would just be time for the initial flight tests and Lloyd's certification in the closing months of 2060 before *Universe* left Earth orbit for her rendezvous. It would be a very close thing: Halley's comet would not wait, even for Sir Lawrence Tsung.

9 · Mount Zeus

The survey satellite Europa VI had been in orbit for almost fifteen years and had far exceeded its design life; whether it should be replaced was a subject of considerable debate in the small Ganymede scientific establishment.

It carried the usual collection of data-gathering instruments, as well as a now-virtually-useless imaging system. Though still in perfect working order, all that this normally showed of Europa was an unbroken cloudscape. The overworked science team on Ganymede scanned the recordings in Quick Look mode once a week, then squirted the raw data back to Earth. On the whole, they would be rather relieved when Europa VI expired and its torrent of uninteresting gigabytes finally dried up.

Now, for the first time in years, it had produced something exciting.

"Orbit 71934," said the deputy chief astronomer, who had called van der Berg as soon as the latest data dump had been evaluated. "Coming in from the Nightside—heading straight for Mount Zeus. You won't see anything for another ten seconds, though."

The screen was completely black, yet van der Berg could imagine the frozen landscape rolling past beneath its blanket of clouds a thousand kilometers below. In a few hours the distant Sun would be shining there, for Europa revolved on its axis once in every seven Earth-days. "Nightside" should really be called "Twilight-side", for half the time it had ample light—but no heat. Yet the inaccurate name had stuck, because it had emotional validity: Europa knew Sunrise, but never Lucifer-rise.

And the Sunrise was coming now, speeded up a thousandfold by the racing probe. A faintly luminous band bisected the screen as the horizon emerged from darkness.

The explosion of light was so sudden that van der Berg could almost imagine he was looking into the glare of an atomic bomb. In a fraction of a second, it ran through all the colors of the rainbow, then became pure white as the sun leaped above the mountain—then vanished as the automatic filters cut into the circuit.

"That's all; pity there was no operator on duty at the time—he could have panned the camera down and had a good view of the mountain as we went over. But I knew you'd like to see it—even though it disproves your theory."

"How?" said van der Berg, more puzzled than annoyed.

"When you go through it in slow motion, you'll see what I mean. Those beautiful rainbow effects—they're not atmospheric—they're caused *by the mountain itself.* Only ice could do that. Or glass—which doesn't seem very likely."

"Not impossible—volcanoes can produce natural glass—but it's usually black . . . of course!"

"Yes?"

"Er—I won't commit myself until I've been through the data. But my guess would be rock crystal—transparent quartz. You can make beautiful prisms and lenses out of it. Any chance of some more observations?"

"I'm afraid not—that was pure luck—Sun, mountain, camera all lined up at the right time. It won't happen again in a thousand years."

"Thanks, anyway—can you send me over a copy? No hurry—I'm just leaving on a field trip to Perrine, and won't be able to look at it until I get back." van der Berg gave a short, rather apologetic laugh. "You know, if that really *is* rock crystal, it would be worth a fortune. Might even help solve our balance of payments problem . . ."

But that, of course, was utter fantasy. Whatever wonders—or treasures—Europa might conceal, the human race had been forbidden access to them by that last message from *Discovery.* Fifty years later, there was no sign that the interdiction would ever be lifted.

10 · Ship of Fools

For the first forty-eight hours of the voyage, Heywood Floyd could not really believe the comfort, the spaciousness—the sheer *extravagance* of *Universe*'s living arrangements. Yet most of his fellow passengers took them for granted; those who had never left Earth before assumed that *all* spaceships must be like this.

He had to look back at the history of aeronautics to put matters in the right perspective. In his own lifetime, he had witnessed—indeed, experienced—the revolution that had occurred in the skies of the planet now dwindling behind him. Between the clumsy old *Leonov* and the sophisticated *Universe* lay exactly fifty years. (Emotionally, he couldn't *really* believe that—but it was useless arguing with arithmetic.)

And just fifty years had separated the Wright Brothers from the first jet airliners. At the beginning of that half century, intrepid aviators had hopped from field to field, begoggled and windswept on open chairs; at its end, grandmothers had slumbered peacefully between continents at a thousand kilometers an hour.

So he should not, perhaps, have been astonished at the luxury and elegant decor of his stateroom, or even the fact that he had a steward to keep it tidy. The generously sized window was the most startling feature of his suite, and at first he felt quite uncomfortable thinking of the tons of air pressure it was holding in check against the implacable, and never for a moment relaxing, vacuum of space.

The biggest surprise, even though the advance literature should have prepared him for it, was the presence of gravity. *Universe* was the first spaceship ever built to cruise under continuous acceleration, except for the few hours of the midcourse turnaround. When her huge propellant tanks were fully loaded with their five thousand tons of water, she could manage a tenth of a gee—not much, but enough to keep loose objects from drifting around. This was particularly convenient at mealtimes—though it took a few days for the passengers to learn not to stir their soup too vigorously.

Forty-eight hours out from Earth, the population of *Universe* had already stratified itself into four distinct classes.

The aristocracy consisted of Captain Smith and his officers. Next came the passengers; then crew—noncommissioned and stewards. And then steerage . . .

That was the description that the five young space scientists had adopted for themselves, first as a joke but later with a certain amount of bitterness. When Floyd compared their cramped and jury-rigged quarters with his own luxurious cabin, he could see their point of view, and soon became the conduit of their complaints to the captain.

Yet all things considered, they had little to grumble about; in the rush to get the ship ready, it had been touch and go as to whether there would be *any* accommodation for them and their equipment. Now they could look forward to deploying instruments around—and *on*—the comet during the critical days before it rounded the Sun and departed once more to the outer reaches of the Solar System. The members of the science team would establish their reputations on this voyage, and knew it. Only in moments of exhaustion, or fury with misbehaving instrumentation, did they start complaining about the noisy ventilating system, the claustrophobic cabins, and occasional strange smells of unknown origin.

But never the food, which everyone agreed was excellent. "Much better," Captain Smith assured them, "than Darwin had on the *Beagle*."

To which Victor Willis had promptly retorted: "How does *he* know? And by the way, *Beagle*'s commander cut his throat when he got back to England."

That was rather typical of Victor, perhaps the planet's best-known science communicator (to his fans) or pop scientist (to his equally numerous detractors). It would be unfair to call them enemies; admiration for his talents was universal, if occasionally grudging). His soft, mid-Pacific accent and expansive gestures on camera were widely parodied, and he had been credited (or blamed) for the revival of full-length beards. "A man who grows *that* much hair," critics were fond of saying, "must have a lot to hide."

He was certainly the most instantly recognizable of the six VIPS—though Floyd, who no longer regarded himself as a celebrity, always referred to them ironically as "The Famous Five." Yva Merlin could often walk unrecognized on Park Avenue, on the rare occasions when she emerged from her apartment. Dimitri Mihailovich, to his considerable annoyance, was a good ten centimeters below average height; this might help to explain his fondness for thousand-piece orchestras—real or synthesized—but did not enhance his public image.

Clifford Greenberg and Margaret M'Bala also fell into the category of "famous unknowns"—though this would certainly change when they got back to Earth. The first man to land on Mercury had one of those pleasant, unremarkable faces that are very hard to remember; moreover, the days when he had dominated the news were now thirty years in the past. And like most authors who are not addicted to talk shows and autographing sessions, Ms. M'Bala would be unrecognized by the vast majority of her millions of readers.

Her literary fame had been one of the sensations of the '40s. A scholarly study of the Greek pantheon was not usually a candidate for the bestseller lists, but Ms. M'Bala had placed its eternally inexhaustible myths in the contemporary space-age setting. Names that a century earlier had been familiar only to astronomers and classical scholars were now part of every educated person's world picture; almost every day there would be news from Ganymede, Callisto, Io, Titan, Iapetus—or even more obscure worlds like Carme, Pasiphae, Hyperion, Phoebe . . .

Her book would have been no more than modestly successful, however, had she not focused on the complicated family life of Jupiter-Zeus, Father of all the Gods (as well as much else). And by a stroke of luck, an editor of genius had changed her original title, *The View From Olympus,* to *The Passions of the Gods.* Envious academics usually referred to it as *Olympic Lusts,* but invariably wished they had written it.

Not surprisingly, it was Maggie M—as she was quickly christened by her fellow passengers—who first used the phrase *Ship of Fools.* Victor Willis adopted it eagerly, and soon discovered an intriguing historical resonance. Almost a century ago, Katherine Anne Porter had herself sailed with a group of scientists and writers aboard an ocean liner to watch the launch of *Apollo 17* and the end of the first phase of lunar exploration.

"I'll think about it," Ms. M'Bala had remarked ominously, when this was reported to her. "Perhaps it's time for a third version. But I won't know, of course, until we get back to Earth . . . ."

11 · The Lie

It was many months before Rolf van der Berg could once again turn his thoughts and energies toward Mount Zeus. The taming of Ganymede was a more than full-time job, and he was away from his main office at Dardanus Base for weeks at a time, surveying the route of the proposed Gilgamesh–Osiris monorail.

The geography of the third and largest Galilean moon had changed drastically since the detonation of Jupiter—and it was still changing. The new sun that had melted the ice of Europa was not as powerful here, four hundred thousand kilometers farther out—but it was warm enough to produce a temperate climate at the center of the face forever turned toward it. There were small, shallow seas—some as large as Earth's Mediterreanean—up to latitudes forty north and south. Not many features still survived from the maps generated by the Voyager missions back in the twentieth century. Melting permafrost and occasional tectonic movements triggered by the same tidal forces operating on the two inner moons made the new Ganymede a cartographer's nightmare.

But those very factors also made it a planetary engineer's paradise. Here was the only world, except for the arid and much-less-hospitable Mars, on which men might one day walk unprotected beneath an open sky. Ganymede had ample water, all the chemicals of life, and—at least while Lucifer shone—a warmer climate than much of Earth.

Best of all, full-body spacesuits were no longer necessary; the atmosphere, though still unbreathable, was just dense enough to permit the use of simple facemasks and oxygen cylinders. In a few decades—so the microbiologists promised, though they were hazy about specific dates—even these could be discarded. Strains of oxygen-generating bacteria had already been let loose across the face of Ganymede; most had died but some had flourished, and the slowly rising curve on the atmospheric analysis chart was the first exhibit proudly displayed to all visitors at Dardanus.

For a long time, van der Berg kept a watchful eye on the data flowing in from Europa VI, hoping that one day the clouds would clear again when it was orbiting above Mount Zeus. He knew that the odds were against it, but while the slightest chance existed he made no effort to explore any other avenue of research. There was no hurry, he had far more important work on his hands—and anyway, the explanation might turn out to be something quite trivial and uninteresting.

Then Europa VI suddenly expired, almost certainly as a result of a random meteoric impact. Back on Earth, Victor Willis had made rather a fool of himself—in the opinion of many—by interviewing the "Euronuts" who now more-than-adequately filled the gap left by the UFO-enthusiasts of the previous century. Some of them argued that the probe's demise was due to hostile action from the world below: the fact that it had been allowed to operate without interference for fifteen years—almost twice its design life—did not bother them in the least. To Victor's credit, he stressed this point and demolished most of the cultist's other arguments: but the consensus was that he should never have given them publicity in the first place.

To van der Berg, who quite relished his colleagues' description of him as a "stubborn Dutchman" and did his best to live up to it, the failure of Europa VI was a challenge not to be resisted. There was not the slightest hope of funding a replacement, for the silencing of the garrulous and embarrassingly long-lived probe had been received with considerable relief.

So what was the alternative? van der Berg sat down to consider his options. Because he was a geologist and not an astrophysicist, it was several days before he suddenly realized that the answer had been staring him in the face ever since he had landed on Ganymede.

Afrikaans is one of the world's best languages in which to curse; even when spoken politely, it can bruise innocent bystanders. van der Berg let off steam for a few minutes; then he put through a call to the Tiamat Observatory—sitting precisely on the Equator, with the tiny, blinding disk of Lucifer forever vertically overhead.

Astrophysicists, concerned with the most spectacular objects in the Universe, tend to patronize mere geologists, who devote their lives to small, messy things like planets. But out here on the frontier, everyone helped everyone else, and Dr. Wilkins was not only interested but sympathetic.

The Tiamat Observatory had been built for a single purpose, which had indeed been one of the main reasons for establishing a base on Ganymede.

The study of Lucifer was of enormous importance not only to pure scientists but also to nuclear engineers, meteorologists, oceanographers—and, not least, to statesmen and philosophers. That there were entities who could turn a planet into a sun was a staggering thought, and had kept many awake at night. It would be well for Mankind to learn all it could about the process; one day there might be need to imitate it—or prevent it . . .

And so for more than a decade Tiamat had been observing Lucifer with every possible type of instrumentation, continually recording its spectrum across the entire electromagnetic band and also actively probing it with radar from a modest hundredmeter dish slung across a small impact crater.

"Yes," said Dr. Wilkins, "we've often looked at Europa and Io. But our beam is fixed on Lucifer, so we can only see them for a few minutes while they're in transit. And your Mount Zeus is just on the dayside—so it's always hidden then."

"I realize *that*," said van der Berg a little impatiently. "But couldn't you offset the beam by just a little, so you could have a look at Europa before it comes in line? Ten or twenty degrees would get you far enough into Dayside."

"*One* degree would be enough to miss Lucifer and get Europa full-face on the other side of its orbit. But then it would be more than three times farther away, so we'd only have a hundredth of the reflected power. Might work, though: we'll give it a try. Let me have the specs on frequencies, wave envelopes, polarization, and anything else your remote-sensing people think will help. It won't take us long to rig up a phase-shifting network that will slew the beam a couple of degrees. More than that I don't know— it's not a problem we've ever considered. Though perhaps we should have done so—anyway, what do you expect to find on Europa, except ice and water?"

"If I knew," said van der Berg cheerfully, "I wouldn't be asking for help, would I?"

"And *I* wouldn't be asking for full credit when you publish. Too bad my name's at the end of the alphabet; you'll be ahead of me by only one letter."

That was a year ago: the long-range scans hadn't been good enough, and offsetting the beam to look onto Europa's day side just before conjunction had proved more difficult than expected. But at last the results were in; the computers had digested them, and van der Berg was the first human being to look at a minerological map of post-Lucifer Europa.

It was, as Dr. Wilkins had surmised, mostly ice and water, with outcroppings of basalt interspersed with deposits of sulfur. But there were two anomalies.

One appeared to be an artifact of the imaging process; there was an absolutely straight feature, two kilometers long, that showed virtually no radar echo. van der Berg left Dr. Wilkins to puzzle over that: he was concerned only with Mount Zeus.

It had taken him a long time to make the identification, because only a madman—or a really desperate scientist—would have dreamed that such a thing was possible. Even now, though every parameter checked to the limits of accuracy, he still could not really believe it. And he had not even attempted to consider his next move.

When Dr. Wilkins called, anxious to see his name and reputation spreading through the data banks, he mumbled that he was still analyzing the results. But at last he could put it off no longer.

"Nothing very exciting," he told his unsuspecting colleague. "Merely a rare form of quartz—I'm still trying to match it from Earth samples."

It was the first time he had ever lied to a fellow scientist, and he felt terrible about it.

But what was the alternative?

12 · Oom Paul

Rolf van der Berg had not seen his Uncle Paul for a decade, and it was not likely that they would ever again meet in the flesh. Yet he felt very close to the old scientist—the last of his generation, and only one who could recall (when he wished, which was seldom) his forefathers' way of life.

Dr. Paul Kreuger—"Oom Paul" to all his family and most of his friends —was always there when he was needed, with information and advice, either in person or at the end of a half-billion-kilometer radio link. Rumor had it that only extreme political pressure had forced the Nobel Committee to overlook his contributions to particle physics, now once more in desperate disarray after the general housecleaning at the end of the twentieth century.

If this was true, Dr. Kreuger bore no grudge. Modest and unassuming, he had no personal enemies, even among the cantankerous factions of his fellow exiles. Indeed, he was so universally respected that he had received several invitations to revisit the United States of Southern Africa, but had always politely declined—not, he hastened to explain, because he felt he would be in any physical danger in the USSA, but because he feared that the sense of nostalgia would be overwhelming.

Even using the security of a language now understood by less than a million people, van der Berg had been very discreet, and had used circumloquations and references that would be meaningless except to a close relative. But Paul had no difficulty in understanding his nephew's message, though he could not take it seriously. He was afraid young Rolf had made a fool of himself, and would let him down as gently as possible. Just as well he hadn't rushed to publish: at least he had the sense to keep quiet . . .

And suppose—just suppose—it *was* true? The scanty hairs rose on the back of Paul's head. A whole spectrum of possibilities—scientific, financial, political—suddenly opened up before his eyes, and the more he considered them, the more awesome they appeared.

Unlike his devout ancestors, Dr. Kreuger had no God to address in moments of crisis or perplexity. Now he almost wished he had: but even if he could pray, that wouldn't really help. As he sat down at his computer and started to access the data banks, he did not know whether to hope that his nephew had made a stupendous discovery—or was talking utter nonsense. Could the Old One *really* play such an incredible trick on mankind? Paul remembered Einstein's famous comment that though He was subtle, He was never malicious.

Stop daydreaming, Dr. Paul Kreuger told himself. *Your* likes or dislikes, *your* hopes or fears, have absolutely nothing to do with the matter . . .

A challenge had been flung to him across half the width of the Solar System; he would not know peace until he had uncovered the truth.

13 · "No One Told Us To Bring Swimsuits . . ."

Captain Smith kept his little surprise until Day 5, just a few hours before Turnaround. His announcement was received, as he had expected, with stunned incredulity.

Victor Willis was the first to recover.

"A *swimming pool!* In a spaceship! You must be joking!"

The captain leaned back and prepared to enjoy himself. He grinned at Heywood Floyd, who had already been let into the secret.

"Well, I suppose Columbus would have been amazed at some of the facilities on the ships that came after him."

"Is there a diving board?" asked Greenberg wistfully. "I used to be college champion."

"As a matter of fact—yes. It's only five meters—but that will give you three seconds of free fall at our nominal tenth of a gee. And if you want a longer time, I'm sure Mr. Curtis will be happy to reduce thrust."

"Indeed?" said the chief engineer dryly. "And mess up all my orbit calculations? Not to mention the risk of the water crawling out. Surface tension, you know . . ."

"Wasn't there a space station once that had a *spherical* swimming pool?" somebody asked.

"They tried it at the hub of Pasteur, before they started the spin," answered Floyd. "It just wasn't practical. In zero gravity, it had to be completely enclosed. And you could drown rather easily inside a big sphere of water, if you panicked."

"One way of getting into the record books—first person to drown in space—"

"No one told us to bring swimsuits," complained Maggie M'Bala.

"Anyone who *has* to wear a swimsuit probably should," Mihailovich whispered to Floyd.

Captain Smith rapped on the table to restore order.

"This is more important, please. As you know, at midnight we reach maximum speed and have to start braking. So the drive will shut down at 2300, and the ship will be reversed. We'll have two hours of weightlessness before we commence thrust again at 0100.

"As you can imagine, the crew will be rather busy—we'll use the opportunity for an engine check and a hull inspection, which can't be done while we're under power. I strongly advise you to be sleeping then, with the restraint straps lightly fastened across your beds. The stewards will check that there aren't any loose articles that could cause trouble when weight comes on again. Questions?"

There was a profound silence, as if the assembled passengers were still somewhat stunned by the revelation and were deciding what to do about it.

"I was hoping you'd ask me about the economics of such a luxury—but as you haven't, I'll tell you anyway. It's not a luxury at all—it doesn't cost a thing, but we hope it will be a very valuable asset on future voyages.

"You see, we have to carry five thousand tons of water as reaction mass, so we might as well make the best use of it. Number One tank is now three-quarters empty; we'll keep it that way until the end of the voyage. So after breakfast tomorrow—see you down at the beach . . ."

Considering the rush to get *Universe* spaceborne, it was surprising that such a good job had been done on something so spectacularly nonessential.

The "beach" was a metal platform, about five meters wide, curving around a third of the great tank's circumference. Although the far wall was only another twenty meters away, clever use of projected images made it seem at infinity. Borne on the waves in the middle distance, surfers were heading toward a shore which they would never reach. Beyond them, a beautiful passenger clipper that any travel agent would recognize instantly as Tsung Sea-Space Corporation's *Tai-Pan* was racing along the horizon under a full spread of sail.

To complete the illusion, there was sand underfoot (slightly magnetized, so it would not stray too far from its appointed place), and the short length of beach ended in a grove of palm trees that were quite convincing, until examined too closely. Overhead, a hot tropical sun completed the idyllic picture; it was hard to realize that just beyond these walls the *real* Sun was shining, now twice as fiercely as on any terrestrial beach.

The designer had really done a wonderful job in the limited space available. It seemed a little unfair of Greenberg to complain, "Pity there's no surf."

14 · Search

It is a good principle in science not to believe any "fact"—however well attested—until it fits into some accepted frame of reference. Occasionally, of course, an observation can shatter the frame and force the construction of a new one, but that is extremely rare. Galileos and Einsteins seldom appear more than once per century, which is just as well for the equanimity of mankind.

Dr. Kreuger fully accepted this principle: he would not believe his nephew's discovery until he could explain it, and as far as he could see that required nothing less than a direct act of God. Wielding Occam's still highly serviceable razor, he thought it somewhat more probable that Rolf had made a mistake; if so, it should be fairly easy to find it.

To Uncle Paul's great surprise, it proved very difficult indeed. The analysis of radar remote-sensing observations was now a venerable and well-established art, and the experts that Paul consulted all gave the same answer, after considerable delay. They also asked: "Where *did* you get that recording?"

"Sorry," he had answered. "I'm not at liberty to say."

The next step was to assume that the impossible was correct, and to start searching the literature. This could be an enormous job, for he did not even know where to begin. One thing was quite certain: a brute-force, head-on attack was bound to fail. It would be just as if Roentgen, the morning after he had discovered X-rays, had started to hunt for their explanation in the physics journals of his day. The information he needed still lay years in the future.

But there was at least a sporting chance that what he was looking for was hidden somewhere in the immense body of existing scientific knowledge. Slowly and carefully, Paul Kreuger set up an automatic search program designed for what it would exclude as much as what it would embrace. It should cut out all Earth-related references—they would certainly number in the millions—and concentrate entirely on extraterrestrial citations.

One of the benefits of Dr. Kreuger's eminence was an unlimited computer budget: that was part of the fee he demanded from the various organizations that needed his wisdom. Though this search might be expensive, he did not have to worry about the bill.

As it turned out, this was surprisingly small. He was lucky: the search came to an end after only two hours thirty-seven minutes, at the 21,456th reference.

The title was enough. Paul was so excited that his own comsec refused to recognize his voice, and he had to repeat the command for a full printout.

Nature had published the paper in 1981—almost five years before he was born!—and as his eyes swept swiftly over its single page he knew not only that his nephew had been right all along—but, just as important, exactly how such a miracle could occur.

The editor of that eighty-year-old journal must have had a good sense of humor. A paper discussing the cores of the outer planets was not something to grab the casual reader: this one, however, had an unusually striking title. His comsec could have told him quickly enough that it had once been part of a famous song, but that of course was quite irrelevant.

Anyway, Paul Kreuger had never heard of the Beatles and their psychedelic fantasies.

II
The
Valley
of
Black
Snow

15 · Rendezvous

And now Halley was too close to be seen; ironically, observers back on Earth would get a far better view of the tail, already stretching fifty million kilometers at right angles to the comet's orbit, like a pennant fluttering in the invisible gale of the solar wind.

On the morning of the rendezvous, Heywood Floyd woke early from a troubled sleep. It was unusual for him to dream—or at least to remember his dreams—and doubtless the anticipated excitements of the next few hours were responsible. He was also slightly worried by a message from Caroline, asking if he had heard from Chris lately. He had radioed back, a little tersely, that Chris had never bothered to say "Thank you" when he had helped him get his current position on *Universe*'s sister ship *Cosmos*; perhaps he was already bored with the Earth–Moon run and was looking for excitement elsewhere.

"As usual," Floyd had added, "we'll hear from him in his own good time."

Immediately after breakfast, passengers and science team had gathered for a final briefing from Captain Smith. The scientists certainly did not need it, but if they felt any irritation, so childish an emotion would have been quickly swept away by the weird spectacle on the main viewscreen.

It was easier to imagine that *Universe* was flying into a nebula rather than a comet. The entire sky ahead was now a misty white fog—not uniform, but mottled with darker condensations and streaked with luminous bands and brightly glowing jets, all radiating away from a central point. At this magnification, the nucleus was barely visible as a tiny black speck, yet it was clearly the source of all the phenomena around it.

"We cut our drive in three hours," said the captain. "Then we'll be only a thousand kilometers away from the nucleus, with virtually zero velocity. We'll make some final observations, and confirm our landing site.

"So we'll go weightless at 1200 exactly. Before then, your cabin stewards will check that everything's correctly stowed. It will be just like Turn-around, except that *this* time it's going to be three days, not two hours, before we have weight again.

"Halley's gravity? Forget it—less than one centimeter per second squared—just about a thousandth of Earth's. You'll be able to detect it if you wait long enough, but that's about all. Takes fifteen seconds for something to fall a meter.

"For safety, I'd like you all here in the observation lounge, with your seat belts properly secured, during rendezvous and touchdown. You'll get the best view from here, anyway, and the whole operation won't take more than an hour. We'll only be using very small thrust corrections, but they may come from any angle and could cause minor sensory disturbances."

What the captain meant, of course, was spacesickness—but that word, by general agreement, was taboo aboard *Universe.* It was noticeable, however, that many hands strayed into the compartments beneath the seats, as if checking that the notorious plastic bags would be available if urgently required.

The image on the viewscreen expanded as the magnification was increased. For a moment it seemed to Floyd that he was in an airplane, descending through light clouds, rather than in a spacecraft approaching the most famous of all comets. The nucleus was growing larger and clearer; it was no longer a black dot, but an irregular ellipse—now a small, pockmarked island lost in the cosmic ocean—then, suddenly, a world in its own right.

There was still no sense of scale. Although Floyd knew that the whole panorama spread before him was less than ten kilometers across, he could easily have imagined that he was looking at a body as large as the Moon. But the Moon was not hazy around the edges, nor did it have little jets of vapor—and two large ones—spurting from its surface.

"My God!" cried Mihailovich, "what's *that?*"

He pointed to the lower edge of the nucleus, just inside the terminator. Unmistakably—impossibly—a light was flashing there on the nightside of the comet with a perfectly regular rhythm: on, off, on, off, once every two or three seconds.

Dr. Willis gave his patent "I can explain it to you in words of one syllable" cough, but Captain Smith got there first.

"I'm sorry to disappoint you, Mr. Mihailovich. That's only the beacon on Sampler Probe Two. It's been sitting there for a month, waiting for us to come and pick it up."

"What a shame; I thought there might be someone—something—there to welcome us."

"No such luck, I'm afraid; we're very much on our own out here. That beacon is just where we intend to land—it's near Halley's South Pole and is in permanent darkness at the moment. That will make it easier on our life-support systems. The temperature's up to 120 degrees on the sunlit side—way above boiling point."

"No wonder the comet's perking," said the unabashed Dimitri. "Those jets don't look very healthy to me. Are you sure it's safe to go in?"

"That's another reason we're touching down on the night side; there's no activity there. Now, if you'll excuse me, I must get back to the bridge. This is the first chance I've ever had of landing on a new world—and I doubt if I'll get another."

Captain Smith's audience dispersed slowly, and in unusual silence. The image on the viewscreen zoomed back to normal, and the nucleus dwindled once more to a barely visible spot. Yet even in these few minutes it seemed to have grown slightly larger, and perhaps that was no illusion. Less than four hours before encounter, the ship was still hurtling toward the comet at fifty thousand kilometers an hour.

It would make a crater more impressive than any that Halley now boasted if something happened to the main drive at this stage of the game.

16 · Touchdown

The landing was just as anticlimatic as Captain Smith had hoped. It was impossible to tell the moment when *Universe* made contact; a full minute elapsed before the passengers realized that touchdown was complete, and raised a belated cheer.

The ship lay at one end of a shallow valley surrounded by hills little more than a hundred meters high. Anyone who had been expecting to see a lunar landscape would have been greatly surprised; these formations bore no resemblance at all to the smooth, gentle slopes of the Moon, sand-blasted by micrometeorite bombardment over billions of years.

There was nothing here more than a thousand years old; the pyramids were far more ancient than this landscape. Every time around the Sun, Halley was remolded—and diminished—by the solar fires. Even since the 1986 perihelion passage, the shape of the nucleus had been subtly changed. Melding metaphors shamelessly, Victor Willis had nevertheless put it rather well when he told his viewers: "The 'peanut' has become wasp-waisted!" Indeed, there were indications that, after a few more revolutions round the Sun, Halley might split into two roughly equal fragments—as had Biela's comet, to the amazement of the astronomers of 1846.

The virtually nonexistent gravity also contributed to the strangeness of the landscape. All around were spidery formations like the fantasies of a surrealist artist and improbably canted rockpiles that could not have survived more than a few minutes even on the Moon.

Although Captain Smith had chosen to land *Universe* in the depths of the polar night—all of five kilometers from the blistering heat of the Sun—there was ample illumination. The huge envelope of gas and dust surrounding the comet formed a glowing halo that seemed appropriate for this region; it was easy to imagine that it was an aurora, playing over the Antarctic ice. And if that was not sufficient, Lucifer provided its quota of several hundred full Moons.

Although expected, the complete absence of color was a disappointment; *Universe* might have been sitting in an opencast coal mine: that, in fact, was not a bad analogy, for much of the surrounding blackness was due to carbon or its compounds, intimately mixed with snow and ice.

Captain Smith, as was his due, was the first to leave the ship, pushing himself gently out from *Universe*'s main airlock. It seemed an eternity before he reached the ground, two meters below; then he picked up a handful of the powdery surface and examined it in his gloved hand.

Aboard the ship, everyone waited for the words that would go into the history books.

"Looks like pepper and salt," said the captain. "If it was thawed out, it might grow a pretty good crop."

The mission plan involved one complete Halley "day" of fifty-five hours at the South Pole, then—if there were no problems—a move of ten kilometers toward the very ill-defined Equator, to study one of the geysers during a complete day-night cycle.

Chief Scientist Pendrill wasted no time. Almost immediately, he set off with a colleague on a two-man jet sled toward the beacon of the waiting probe. They were back within the hour, bearing prepackaged samples of comet that they proudly consigned to the deep freeze.

Meanwhile the other teams established a spider's web of cables along the valley, strung between poles driven into the friable crust. These served not only to link numerous instruments to the ship, but also made movement outside much easier. One could explore this portion of Halley without the use of cumbersome External Maneuvering Units; it was only necessary to attach a tether to a cable, and then go along it hand over hand. That was also much more fun than operating EMUs, which were virtually one-man spaceships, with all the complications they involved.

The passengers watched all this with fascination, listening to the radioed conversations and trying to join in the excitement of discovery. After about twelve hours—considerably less in the case of exastronaut Clifford Greenberg—the pleasure of being a captive audience started to pall. Soon there was much talk about "going outside"—except from Victor Willis, who was quite uncharacteristically subdued.

"I think he's scared," said Dimitri contemptuously. He had never liked Victor, since discovering that the scientist was completely tone deaf. Though this was wildly unfair to Victor (who had gamely allowed himself to be used as a guinea pig for studies of his curious affliction), Dimitri was fond of adding darkly "A man that hath no music in himself, Is fit for treasons, strategems and spoils."

Floyd had made up his mind even before leaving Earth orbit. Maggie M was game enough to try anything and would need no encouragement (her slogan "An author should never turn down the opportunity for a new experience" had impacted famously on her emotional life).

Yva Merlin, as usual, had kept everyone in suspense, but Floyd was determined to take her on a personal tour of the comet. It was the very least he could do to maintain his reputation; everyone knew that he had been partly responsible for getting the fabulous recluse on the passenger list, and now it was a running joke that they were having an affair. Their most innocent remarks were gleefully misinterpreted by Dimitri and the ship's physician, Dr. Mahindran, who professed to regard them with envious awe.

After some initial annoyance—because it all too accurately recalled the emotions of his youth—Floyd had gone along with the joke. But he did not know how Yva felt about it and had so far lacked the courage to ask her. Even now, in this compact little society where few secrets lasted more than six hours, she maintained much of her famous reserve—that aura of mystery which had fascinated audiences for three generations.

As for Victor Willis, he had just discovered one of those devastating little details that can destroy the best-laid plans of mice and spacemen.

Universe was equipped with the latest Mark XX suits, with nonfogging, nonreflective visors guaranteed to give an unparalleled view of space. And though the helmets came in several sizes, Victor Willis could not get into any of them without major surgery.

It had taken him fifteen years to perfect his trademark ("A triumph of the topiary art," one critic had called it, perhaps admiringly).

Now only his beard stood between Victor Willis and Halley's Comet. Soon he would have to make a choice between the two.

17 · The Valley of Black Snow

Captain Smith had raised surprisingly few objections to the idea of passenger EVAs. He agreed that to have come all this way and not to set foot upon the comet was absurd.

"There'll be no problems if you follow instructions," he said at the inevitable briefing. "Even if you've never worn spacesuits before—and I believe that only Commander Greenberg and Dr. Floyd have done so—they're quite comfortable, and fully automatic. There's no need to bother about any controls or adjustments, after you've been checked out in the airlock.

"One absolute rule: only two of you can go EVA at one time. You'll have a personal escort, of course, linked to you by five meters of safety line—though that can be played out to twenty if necessary. In addition, you'll *both* be tethered to the two guide cables we've strung the whole length of the valley. The rule of the road is the same as on Earth: keep to the right! If you want to overtake anyone, you only have to unclip your buckle—but *one* of you must always remain attached to the line. That way, there's no danger of drifting off onto space. Any questions?"

"How long can we stay out?"

"As long as you like, Miz M'Bala. But I recommend that you return just as soon as you feel the slightest discomfort. Perhaps an hour would be best for the first outing—though it may seem like only ten minutes . . ."

Captain Smith had been quite correct. As Heywood Floyd looked at his time-elapsed display, it seemed incredible that forty minutes had already passed. Yet it should not have been so surprising, for the ship was already a good kilometer away.

As the senior passenger—by almost any reckoning—he had been given the privilege of making the first EVA. And he really had no choice of companion.

"EVA with Yva!" chortled Mihailovich. "How can you possibly resist! Even if"—he added with a lewd grin—"those damn suits won't let you try all the extravehicular activities you'd like."

Yva had agreed, without any hesitation, yet also without any enthusiasm. That, Floyd thought wryly, was typical. It would not be quite true to say that he was disillusioned—at his age, he had very few illusions left—but he was disappointed. And with himself rather than Yva; she was as beyond criticism or praise as the Mona Lisa—with whom she had often been compared.

The comparison was, of course, ridiculous; La Gioconda was mysterious, but she was certainly not erotic. Yva's power had lain in her unique combination of both—with innocence thrown in for good measure. Half a century later, traces of all three ingredients were still visible, at least to the eye of faith.

What was lacking—as Floyd had been sadly forced to admit—was any real personality. When he tried to focus his mind upon her, all he could visualize were the roles she had played. He would have reluctantly agreed with the critic who had once said: "Yva Merlin is the reflection of all men's desires; but a mirror has no character."

And now this unique and mysterious creature was floating beside him across the face of Halley's comet, as they and their guide moved along the twin cables that spanned the Valley of Black Snow. That was his name; he was childishly proud of it, even though it would never appear on any map. There could be no maps of a world where geography was as ephemeral as weather on Earth. He savored the knowledge that no human eye had ever before looked upon the scene around him—or ever would again.

On Mars, or on the Moon, you could sometimes—with a slight effort of imagination, and if you ignored the alien sky—pretend that you were on earth. This was impossible here, because the towering—often overhanging —snow sculptures showed only the slightest concession to gravity. You had to look very carefully at your surroundings to decide which way was up.

The Valley of Black Snow was unusual, because it was a fairly solid structure—a rocky reef embedded in volatile drifts of water and hydrocarbon ice. The geologists were still arguing about its origin, some maintaining that it was really part of an asteroid that had encountered the comet ages ago. Corings had revealed complex mixtures of organic compounds, rather like frozen coal-tar—though it was certain that life had never played any part in their formation.

The "snow" carpeting the floor of the little valley was not completely black; when Floyd raked it with the beam of his flashlight it glittered and sparkled as if embedded with a million microscopic diamonds. He wondered if there were indeed diamonds on Halley: there was certainly enough carbon. But it was almost equally certain that the temperatures and pressures necessary to create them had never existed here.

On a sudden impulse, Floyd reached down and gathered two handfuls of the snow: he had to push with his feet against the safety line to do so, and had a comic vision of himself as a trapeze artist walking a tightrope—but upside down. The fragile crust offered virtually no resistance as he buried head and shoulders into it; then he pulled gently on his tether and emerged with his handful of Halley.

As he compacted the mass of crystalline fluff into a ball that just fitted the palm of his hand, he wished that he could *feel* it through the insulation of his gloves. There it lay, ebon black yet giving fugitive flashes of light as he turned it from side to side.

And suddenly, in his imagination, it became the purest white—and he was a boy again, in the winter playground of his youth, surrounded with the ghosts of his childhood. He could even hear the cries of his companions, taunting and threatening him with their own projectiles of immaculate snow . . .

The memory was brief but shattering, for it brought an overwhelming sensation of sadness. Across a century of time, he could no longer remember a single one of those phantom friends who stood around him; yet some, he knew, he had once loved.

His eyes filled with tears, and his fingers clenched around the ball of alien snow. Then the vision faded: he was himself again. This was not a moment of sadness but of triumph.

"My God!" cried Heywood Floyd, his words echoing in the tiny, reverberant universe of his spacesuit. "I'm standing on Halley's comet—what more do I want! If a meteor hits me now, I won't have a single complaint!"

He brought up his arms and launched the snowball toward the stars. It was so small, and so dark, that it vanished almost at once, but he kept on staring into the sky.

And then, abruptly—unexpectedly—it appeared in a sudden explosion of light as it rose into the rays of the hidden sun. Black as soot though it was, it reflected enough of that blinding brilliance to be easily visible against the faintly luminous sky.

Floyd watched it until it finally disappeared—perhaps by evaporation, perhaps by dwindling into the distance. It would not last long in the fierce torrent of radiation overhead; but how many men could claim to have created a comet of their own?

18 · Old Faithful

The cautious exploration of the comet had already begun while *Universe* still remained in the polar shadow. First, one-man EMUs gently jetted over both day and night side, recording everything of interest. Once the preliminary surveys had been completed, groups of up to five scientists flew out in the onboard shuttle, deploying equipment and instruments at strategic spots.

The *Lady Jasmine* was a far cry from the primitive space pods of the *Discovery* era, capable of operating only in a gravity-free environment. She was virtually a small spaceship, designed to ferry personnel and light cargo between the orbiting *Universe* and the surfaces of Mars, Moon, or the Jovian satellites. Her chief pilot, who treated her like the *grande dame* she was, complained with mock bitterness that flying round a miserable little comet was far beneath her dignity.

When Captain Smith was quite sure that Halley—on the surface at least —held no surprises, he lifted away from the pole. Moving less than a dozen kilometers took *Universe* to a different world, from a glimmering twilight that would last for months to a realm that knew the cycle of night and day. And with the dawn, the comet came slowly to life.

As the Sun crept above the jagged, absurdly close horizon, its rays would slant down into the countless small craters that pockmarked the crust. Most of them would remain inactive, their narrow throats sealed by incrustations of mineral salts. Nowhere else on Halley were such vivid displays of color; they had misled biologists into thinking that here life was beginning, as it had on Earth, in the form of algal growths. Many had not yet abandoned that hope, though they would be reluctant to admit it.

From other craters, wisps of vapor floated up into the sky, moving in unnaturally straight trajectories because there were no winds to divert them. Usually nothing else happened for an hour or two; then, as the Sun's warmth penetrated to the frozen interior, Halley would begin to spurt—as Victor Willis had put it—"like a pod of whales."

Though picturesque, it was not one of his more accurate metaphors. The jets from the dayside of Halley were not intermittent, but played steadily for hours at a time. And they did not curl over and fall back to the surface, but went rising on up into the sky, until they were lost in the glowing fog that they helped create.

At first, the science team treated the geysers as cautiously as would vulcanologists approaching Etna or Vesuvius in one of their less predictable moods. But they soon discovered that Halley's eruptions, though often fearsome in appearance, were singularly gentle and well behaved; the water emerged about as fast as from an ordinary firehose, and was barely warm. Within seconds of escaping from its underground reservoir, it would flash into a mixture of vapor and ice crystals; Halley was enveloped in a perpetual snowstorm, falling *upward*. Even at this modest speed of ejection, none of the water would ever return to its source. Each time it rounded the Sun, more of the comet's life-blood would hemorrhage into the insatiable vacuum of space.

After considerable persuasion, Captain Smith agreed to move *Universe* to within a hundred meters of Old Faithful, the largest geyser on the dayside. It was an awesome sight—a whitish-gray column of mist, growing like some giant tree from a surprisingly small orifice in a three-hundred-meter-wide crater that appeared to be one of the oldest formations on the comet. Before long, the scientists were scrambling all over the crater, collecting specimens of its (completely sterile, alas) multicolored minerals and casually thrusting their thermometers and sampling tubes into the soaring water-ice-mist column itself. "If it tosses any of you out into space," warned the captain, "don't expect to be rescued in a hurry. In fact, we may just wait until you come back."

"What does he mean by that?" a puzzled Dimitri Mihailovich had asked. As usual, Victor Willis was quick with the answer.

"Things don't always happen the way you'd expect in celestial mechanics. Anything thrown off Halley at a reasonable speed will still be moving in essentially the same orbit—it takes a *huge* velocity change to make a big difference. So one revolution later, the two orbits will intersect again—and you'll be right back where you started. Seventy-six years older, of course."

Not far from Old Faithful was another phenomenon that no one could reasonably have anticipated. When they first observed it, the scientists could scarcely believe their eyes. Spread out across several hectares of

Halley, exposed to the vacuum of space, was what appeared to be a perfectly ordinary lake, remarkable only for its extreme blackness.

Obviously, it could not be water; the only liquids that could be stable in this environment were heavy organic oils or tars. In fact, Lake Tuonela turned out to be more like pitch, quite solid except for a sticky surface layer less than a millimeter thick. In this negligible gravity, it must have taken years—perhaps several trips round the warming fires of the Sun—for it to have assumed its present mirror-flatness.

Until the captain put a stop to it, the lake became one of the principal tourist attractions on Halley's comet. Someone (nobody claimed the dubious honor) discovered that it was possible to *walk* perfectly normally across it, almost as if on Earth; the surface film had just enough adhesion to hold the foot in place. Before long, most of the crew had got themselves videod apparently walking on water.

Then Captain Smith inspected the airlock, discovered the walls liberally stained with tar, and gave the nearest thing to a display of anger that anyone had ever witnessed.

"It's bad enough," he said through clenched teeth, "having the *outside* of the ship coated with—soot. Halley's comet is about the *filthiest* place I've ever seen."

After that, there were no more strolls on Lake Tuonela.

19 · At the End
of the
Tunnel

Demo

In a small, self-contained universe where everyone knows everyone else, there can be no greater shock than encountering a total stranger.

Heywood Floyd was floating gently along the corridor to the main lounge when he had this disturbing experience. He stared in amazement at the interloper, wondering how a stowaway had managed to avoid detection for so long. The other man looked back at him with a combination of embarrassment and bravado, obviously waiting for Floyd to speak first.

"Well, Victor!" Floyd said at last. "Sorry I didn't recognize you. So you've made the supreme sacrifice for the cause of science—or should I say your public?"

"Yes," Willis answered grumpily. "I *did* manage to squeeze into one helmet—but the damn bristles made so many scratching noises no one could hear a word I said."

"When are you going out?"

"Just as soon as Cliff comes back—he's gone caving with Bill Chant."

The first flybys of the comet, in 1986, had suggested that it was considerably less dense than water—which could only mean that it was either made of very porous material or was riddled with cavities. Both explanations turned out to be correct.

At first, the ever-cautious Captain Smith flatly forbade any cave exploring. He finally relented when Dr. Pendrill reminded him that his chief assistant, Dr. Chant, was an experienced speleologist—indeed, that was one of the very reasons he had been chosen for the mission.

"Cave-ins are impossible in this low gravity," Pendrill had told the reluctant captain. "So there's no danger of being trapped."

"What about being lost?"

"Chant would regard that suggestion as a professional insult. He's been twenty kilometers inside Mammoth Cave. Anyway, he'll play out a guide-line."

"Communications?"

"The line's got fiber optics in it. And suit radio will probably work most of the way."

"Umm. Where does he want to go in?"

"The best place is that extinct geyser at the base of Etna Junior. It's been dead for at least a thousand years."

"So I suppose it should keep quiet for another couple of days. Very well —does anyone else want to go?"

"Cliff Greenberg has volunteered—he's done a good deal of *underwater* cave exploring, in the Bahamas."

"I tried it once—that was enough. Tell Cliff he's much too valuable. He can go in as far as he can still see the entrance—and no further. And if he loses contact with Chant, he's not to go after him without my authority."

Which, the captain added to himself, I would be very reluctant to give.

Dr. Chant knew all the old jokes about speleologists' wanting to return to the womb and was quite sure he could refute them.

"That must be a damn noisy place, with all its thumpings and bumpings and gurglings," he argued. "I love caves because they're so peaceful and timeless. You know that nothing has changed for a hundred thousand years, except that the stalactites have grown a bit thicker."

But now, as he drifted deeper into Halley, playing out the thin but virtually unbreakable thread that linked him to Clifford Greenburg, he realized that this was no longer true. As yet, he had no scientific proof, but his geologist's instincts told him that this subterranean world had been born only yesterday, on the time scale of the Universe. It was younger than some of the cities of Man.

The tunnel through which he was gliding in long, shallow leaps was about four meters in diameter, and his virtual weightlessness brought back vivid memories of cave diving on Earth. The low gravity contributed to the illusion; it was exactly as if he was carrying slightly too much weight, and so kept drifting gently downward. Only the absence of all resistance re-minded him that he was moving through vacuum, not water.

"You're just getting out of sight," said Greenberg, fifty meters in from the entrance. "Radio link still fine. What's the scenery like?"

"Very hard to say—I can't identify any formations, so I don't have the vocabulary to describe them. It's not any kind of rock—it crumbles when I touch it—I feel as if I'm exploring a giant Gruyère cheese . . ."

"You mean it's organic?"

"Yes. Nothing to do with life, of course—but perfect raw material for it. All sorts of hydrocarbons—the chemists will have fun with these samples. Can you still see me?"

"Only the glow of your light, and that's fading fast."

"Ah—here's some genuine rock—doesn't look as if it belongs here—probably an intrusion. Ah—I've struck gold!"

"You're joking!"

"It fooled a lot of people in the old West—iron pyrites. Common on the outer satellites, of course, but don't ask me what it's doing here . . ."

"Visual contact lost. You're two hundred meters in."

"I'm passing through a distinct layer—looks like meteoric debris. Something exciting must have happened back then—I hope we can date it. Wow!"

"Don't do that sort of thing to me!"

"Sorry—quite took my breath away. There's a big chamber ahead—last thing I expected. Let me swing the beam around . . .

"Almost spherical—thirty, forty meters across. And—I don't believe it —Halley *is* full of surprises—stalactites, stalagmites."

"What's so surprising about *that*?"

"No free water, no limestone here, of course—and such low gravity. Looks like some kind of wax. Just a minute while I get good video coverage. Fantastic shapes . . . sort of thing a dripping candle makes. That's odd . . ."

"Now what?"

Dr. Chant's voice had shown a sudden alteration in tone, which Greenburg had instantly detected.

"Some of the columns have been *broken*. They're lying on the floor. It's almost as if . . ."

"Go on!"

"—as if something has—*blundered*—into them."

"That's crazy. Could an earthquake have snapped them?"

"No earthquakes here—only microseisms from the geysers. Perhaps there was a big blow-out at some time. Anyway, it was centuries ago. There's a film of this wax stuff over the fallen columns—several millimeters thick."

Dr. Chant was slowly recovering his composure. He was not a highly imaginative man—spelunking eliminates such people rather quickly—but the very feel of this place had triggered some disturbing memory. And those fallen columns looked altogether too much like the bars of a cage, broken by some monster in an attempt to escape . . .

Of course, that was perfectly absurd—but Dr. Chant had learned never
to ignore any premonition, any danger signal, until he had traced it to its
origin. That caution had saved his life more than once; he would not go
beyond this chamber until he had identified the source of his fear. And he
was honest enough to admit that fear was the correct word.

"Bill—are you all right? What's happening?"

"Still filming. Some of these shapes remind me of Indian temple sculp-
ture. Almost erotic."

He was deliberately turning his mind away from the direct confronta-
tion of his fears, hoping thereby to sneak up on them unawares, by a kind
of averted mental vision. Meanwhile the purely mechanical acts of recording and collecting samples occupied most of his attention.

There was nothing wrong, he reminded himself, with healthy fear; only
when it escalated into panic did it become a killer. He had known panic
twice in his life (once on a mountainside, once underwater) and still shud-
dered at the memory of its clammy touch. Yet—thankfully—he was far
from it now, and for a reason that, though he did not understand it, he
found curiously reassuring. There was an element of *comedy* in the situation.

And presently he started to laugh—not with hysteria, but with relief.

"Did you ever see those old *Star Wars* movies?" he asked Greenberg.

"Of course—half a dozen times."

"Well, I know what's been bothering me. There was a sequence when
Luke's spaceship dives into an asteroid—and runs into a gigantic snake-
creature that lurks inside its caverns."

"Not Luke's ship—Han Solo's *Millennium Falcon*. And I always wondered how that poor beast managed to eke out a living. It must have grown
very hungry, waiting for the occasional tidbit from space. And Princess
Leia wouldn't have been more than a hors d'oeuvre, anyway."

"Which I certainly don't intend to provide," said Dr. Chant, now completely at ease. "Even if there is life here—which would be marvelous—the
food chain would be very short. So I'd be surprised to find anything bigger
than a mouse. Or, more likely, a mushroom . . . Now let's see—where do
we go from here . . . There are two exits on the other side of the chamber. The one on the right is bigger. I'll take that . . ."

"How much more line have you got?"

"Oh, a good half kilometer. Here we go. I'm in the middle of the chamber . . . damn, bounced off the wall. Now I've got a hand-hold . . . going in head first. Smooth walls, real rock for a change . . . That's a
pity . . ."

"What's the problem?"

"Can't go any further. More stalactites . . . too close together for me to
get through . . . and too thick to break without explosives. And that

would be a shame . . . the colors are beautiful—first real greens and blues
I've seen on Halley. Just a minute while I get them on video . . ."

Dr. Chant braced himself against the wall of the narrow tunnel and
aimed the camera. With his gloved fingers he reached for the Hi-intensity
switch, but missed it and cut off the main lights completely.

"Lousy design," he muttered. "Third time I've done that."

He did not immediately correct his mistake, because he had always
enjoyed that silence and total darkness that can be experienced only in the
deepest caves. The gentle background noises of his life-support equipment
robbed him of the silence, but at least—

—what was *that*? From beyond the portcullis of stalactites blocking
further progress he could see a faint glow, like the first light of dawn. As
his eyes grew adapted to the darkness, it appeared to grow brighter, and he
could detect a hint of green. Now he could even see the outlines of the
barrier ahead . . .

"What's happening?" said Greenberg anxiously.

"Nothing—just observing."

And thinking, he might have added. There were four possible explanations.

Sunlight could be filtering down through some natural light duct—ice,
crystal, whatever. But at this depth? Unlikely . . .

Radioactivity? He hadn't bothered to bring a counter; there were virtually no heavy elements here. But it would be worth coming back to check.

Some phosphorescent mineral—that was the one he'd put his money on.
But there was a fourth possibility—the most unlikely, and most exciting,
of all.

Dr. Chant had never forgotten a Moonless—and Luciferless—night on
the shores of the Indian Ocean, when he had been walking beneath brilliant stars along a sandy beach. The sea was very calm, but from time to
time a languid wave would collapse at his feet—and detonate in an explosion of light.

He had walked out into the shallows (he could still remember the feel of
the water round his ankles, like a warm bath) and with every step he took
there had been another burst of light. He could even trigger it by clapping
his hands close to the surface.

Could similar bioluminescent organisms have evolved here in the heart
of Halley's comet? He would love to think so. It seemed a pity to vandalize
something so exquisite as this natural work of art—with the glow behind
it, the barrier now reminded him of an altar screen he had once seen in
some cathedral—but he would have to go back and get some explosives.
Meanwhile, there was the other corridor . . .

"I can't get any further along this route," he told Greenberg, "so I'll try
the other. Coming back to the junction—setting the reel on rewind." He

did not mention the mysterious glow, which had vanished as soon as he switched on his lights again.

Greenberg did not reply immediately, which was unusual; probably he was talking to the ship. Chant did not worry; he would repeat his message as soon as he had got under way again.

He did not bother, because there was a brief acknowledgment from Greenberg.

"Fine, Cliff—thought I'd lost you for a minute. Back at the chamber—now going into the other tunnel. Hope there's nothing blocking *that*."

This time, Greenberg replied at once. "Sorry, Bill. Come back to the ship. There's an emergency—no, not here, everything's fine with *Universe*. But we may have to return to Earth at once."

It was only a few weeks before Dr. Chant discovered a very plausible explanation for the broken columns. As the comet blasted its substance away into space at each perihelion passage, its mass distribution continually altered. And so, every few thousand years, its spin became unstable, and it would change the direction of its axis—quite violently, like a top that is about to fall over as it loses energy. When that occurred, the resulting cometquake could reach a respectable 5 on the Richter scale.

But he never solved the mystery of the luminous glow. Though the problem was swiftly overshadowed by the drama that was now unfolding, the sense of a missed opportunity would continue to haunt him for the rest of his life.

Though he was occasionally tempted, he never mentioned it to any of his colleagues. But he did leave a sealed note for the next expedition, to be opened in 2133.

20 · Recall

"Have you seen Victor?" said Mihailovich gleefully, as Floyd hurried to answer the captain's summons. "He's a broken man."

"He'll grow it back on the way home," snapped Floyd, who had no time for such trivialities at the moment. "I'm trying to find what's happened."

Captain Smith was still sitting, almost stunned, in his cabin when Floyd arrived. If this was an emergency affecting his own ship, he would have been a tornado of controlled energy, issuing orders right and left. But there was nothing he could do about this situation, except await the next message from Earth.

Captain Laplace was an old friend; how *could* he have gotten into such a mess? There was no conceivable accident, error of navigation, or failure of equipment that could possibly account for his predicament. Nor, as far as Smith could see, was there any way in which *Universe* could help him get out of it. Operations Center was just running round and round in circles; this looked like one of those emergencies, all too common in space, where nothing could be done except transmit condolences and record last messages. But he gave no hint of his doubts and reservations when he reported the news to Floyd.

"There's been an accident," he said. "We've received orders to return to Earth immediately, to be fitted out for a rescue mission."

"What kind of accident?"

"It's our sister ship, *Galaxy*. She was doing a survey of the Jovian satellites. And she's made a crash-landing."

He saw the look of amazed incredulity on Floyd's face.

"Yes, I know that's impossible. But you've not heard anything yet. She's stranded—on Europa."

"*Europa*!"

"I'm afraid so. She's damaged, but apparently there's no loss of life. We're still awaiting details."

"When did it happen?"

"Twelve hours ago. There was a delay before she could report to Ganymede."

"But what can *we* do? We're on the other side of the Solar System. Getting back to lunar orbit to refuel, then taking the fastest orbit to Jupiter —it would be—oh, at least a couple of months!" (And back in *Leonov*'s day, Floyd added to himself, it would have been a couple of years . . .)

"I know; but there's no other ship that could do anything."

"What about Ganymede's own intersatellite ferries?"

"They're only designed for orbital operations."

"They've landed on Callisto."

"Much lower energy mission. Oh, they could just manage Europa, but with negligible payload. It's being looked into, of course."

Floyd scarcely heard the captain; he was still trying to assimilate this astonishing news. For the first time in half a century—and only for the second time in all history!—a ship had landed on the forbidden moon. And that prompted an ominous thought.

"Do you suppose," he asked "that—whoever—whatever is on Europa could be responsible?"

"I was wondering about that," said the captain glumly. "But we've been snooping around the place for years without anything happening."

"Even more to the point—what might happen to *us* if we attempted a rescue?"

"That's the first thing that occurred to me. But all this is speculation— we'll have to wait until we have more facts. Meanwhile—this is really why I called you—I've just received *Galaxy*'s crew manifest, and I was wondering . . ."

Hesitantly he pushed the printout across his desk. But even before Heywood Floyd scanned the list, he somehow knew what he would find.

"My grandson," he said bleakly.

And, he added to himself, the only person who can carry my name beyond the grave.

III
Europan
Roulette

21 · The Politics
of Exile

Despite all the gloomier forecasts, the South African Revolution had been comparatively bloodless—as such things go. Television, which had been blamed for many evils, deserved some credit for this. A precedent had been set a generation earlier in the Philippines; when they know that the world is watching, the great majority of men and women tend to behave in a responsible manner. Though there have been shameful exceptions, few massacres occur on camera.

Most of the Afrikaners, when they recognized the inevitable, had left the country long before the take-over of power. And—as the new administration bitterly complained—they had not gone empty-handed. Billions of rands had been transferred to Swiss and Dutch banks; toward the end, there had been mysterious flights almost every hour out of Cape Town and Jo'burg to Zurich and Amsterdam. It was said that by Freedom Day one would not find one Troy ounce of gold or a carat of diamond in the late Republic of South Africa—and the mine workings had been effectively sabotaged. One prominent refugee boasted from his luxury apartment in the Hague, "It will be five years before the Kaffirs can get Kimberley working again—if they ever do." To his great surprise, De Beers was back in business, under new name and management, in less than five weeks, and diamonds were the single most important element in the new nation's economy.

Within a generation, the younger refugees had been absorbed—despite desperate rearguard actions by their conservative elders—in the deracinated culture of the twenty-first century. They recalled, with pride but without boastfulness, the courage and determination of their ancestors, and distanced themselves from their stupidities. Virtually none of them spoke Afrikaans, even in their own homes.

Yet, precisely as in the case of the Russian Revolution a century earlier, there were many who dreamed of putting back the clock—or, at least, of sabotaging the efforts of those who had usurped their power and privilege. Usually they channeled their frustration and bitterness into propaganda, demonstrations, boycotts, petitions to the World Council—and, rarely, works of art. Wilhelm Smuts' *The Voortrekkers* was conceded to be a masterpiece of (ironically) English literature, even by those who bitterly disagreed with the author.

But there were also groups who believed that political action was useless and that only violence would restore the longed-for status quo. Although there could not have been many who really imagined that they could rewrite the pages of history, there were not a few who, if victory was impossible, would gladly settle for revenge.

Between the two extremes of the totally assimilated and the completely intransigent, there was an entire spectrum of political—and apolitical—parties. Der Bund was not the largest, but it was the most powerful, and certainly the richest, since it controlled much of the lost republic's smuggled wealth through a network of corporations and holding companies. Most of these were now perfectly legal and indeed completely respectable.

There was half a billion of Bund money in Tsung Aerospace, duly listed in the annual balance sheet. In 2059, Sir Lawrence was happy to receive another half billion, which enabled him to accelerate the commissioning of his little fleet.

But not even his excellent intelligence traced any connection between the Bund and Tsung Aerospace's latest charter mission for *Galaxy*. In any event, Halley was then approaching Mars, and Sir Lawrence was so busy getting *Universe* ready to leave on schedule that he paid little attention to the routine operations of her sister ships.

Though Lloyds of London did raise some queries about *Galaxy*'s proposed routing, these objections were quickly dealt with. The Bund had people in key positions everywhere; which was unfortunate for the insurance brokers, but very good luck for the space lawyers.

22 · Hazardous Cargo

It is not easy to run a shipping line between destinations that not only change their positions by millions of kilometers every few days, but also swing through a velocity range of tens of kilometers a second. Anything like a regular schedule is out of the question; there are times when one must forget the whole idea and stay in port—or at least in orbit—waiting for the Solar System to rearrange itself for the greater convenience of Mankind.

Fortunately, these periods are known years in advance, so it is possible to make the best use of them for overhauls, retrofits, and planet-leave for the crew. And occasionally, by good luck and aggressive salesmanship, one can arrange some local chartering, even if only the equivalent of the old-time "Once around the Bay" boat ride.

Captain Eric Laplace was delighted that the three-month stayover off Ganymede would not be a complete loss. An anonymous and unexpected grant to the Planetary Science Foundation would finance a reconnaissance of the Jovian (even now, no one ever called it Luciferian) satellite system, paying particular attention to a dozen of the neglected smaller moons. Some of these had never even been properly surveyed, much less visited.

As soon as he heard of the mission, Rolf van der Berg called the Tsung shipping agent and made some discreet inquiries.

"Yes, first we'll head in toward Io—then do a flyby of Europa—"

"Only a flyby? How close?"

"Just a moment—odd, the flight plan doesn't give details. But of course she won't go inside the Interdiction Zone."

"Which was down to ten thousand kilometers at the last ruling . . .

fifteen years ago. Anyway, I'd like to volunteer as mission planetologist.
I'll send across my qualifications . . ."

"No need to do so, Dr. van der Berg. They've already asked for you."

It is always easy to be wise after the event, and when he cast his mind back
(he had plenty of time for it later) Captain Laplace recalled a number of
curious aspects of the charter. Two crew members were suddenly taken
sick and were replaced at short notice; he was so glad to have substitutes
that he did not check their papers as closely as he might have done. (And
even if he had, he would have discovered that they were perfectly in order.)

Then there was the trouble with the cargo. As captain, he was entitled to
inspect anything that went aboard the ship. Of course, it was impossible to
do this for *every* item, but he never hesitated to investigate if he had good
reason. Space crews were, on the whole, a highly responsible body of men;
but long missions could be boring, and there were tedium-relieving chemicals that—though perfectly legal on Earth—should be discouraged off it.

When Second Officer Chris Floyd reported his suspicions, the captain
assumed that the ship's chromatographic sniffer had detected another
cache of the high-grade opium that his largely Chinese crew occasionally
patronized. This time, however, the matter was serious—*very* serious.

"Cargo Hold Three, Item 2/456, Captain. The manifest says "scientific
apparatus." It contains explosives."

"What!"

"Definitely, sir. Here's the electrogram."

"I'll take your word for it, Mr. Floyd. Have you inspected the item?"

"No sir. It's in a sealed case, half a meter by one meter by five meters,
approximately. One of the largest packages the science team brought
aboard. It's labeled FRAGILE—HANDLE WITH CARE. But so is *everything*,
of course."

Captain Laplace drummed his fingers thoughtfully on the grained
plastic "wood" of his desk. (He hated the pattern, and intended to get rid
of it on the next refit.) Even that slight action started him rising out of his
seat, and he automatically anchored himself by wrapping his foot around
the pillar of the chair.

Though he did not for a moment doubt Floyd's report—his new second
officer was very competent, and the captain was pleased that he had never
brought up the subject of his famous grandfather—there could be an innocent explanation. The sniffer might have been misled by other chemicals
with nervous molecular bondings.

They could go down into the hold and force open the package. No—that might be dangerous, and could cause legal problems, as well. Best to go straight to the top; he'd have to do that anyway, sooner or later.

"Please bring Dr. Anderson here—and don't mention this to anyone else."

"Very good, sir." Chris Floyd gave a respectful but quite unnecessary salute, and left the room in a smooth, effortless glide.

The leader of the science team was not accustomed to zero gravity, and his entrance was quite clumsy. His obvious genuine indignation did not help, and he had to grab the captain's desk several times in an undignified manner.

"Explosives! Of course not! Let me see the manifest . . . 2/456 . . ."

Dr. Anderson pecked out the reference on his portable keyboard and slowly read off: ' "Mark V Penetrometers, Quantity Three.' Of course—no problem."

"And just what," said the captain, "is a penetrometer?" Despite his concern, he had difficulty in suppressing a smile; it sounded a little obscene.

"Standard planetary sampling device. You drop it, and with any luck it will give you a core up to ten meters long—even in hard rock. Then it sends back a complete chemical analysis. The only safe way to study places like Dayside Mercury—or Io, where we'll drop the first one."

"Dr. Anderson," said the captain, with great self-restraint, "you may be an excellent geologist, but you don't know much about celestial mechanics. You can't just *drop* things from orbit—"

The charge of ignorance was clearly unfounded, as the scientist's reaction proved.

"The idiots!" he said. "Of course, you should have been notified."

"Exactly. Solid fuel rockets are classified as hazardous cargo. I want clearance from the underwriters, *and* your personal assurance that the safety systems are adequate; otherwise, they go overboard. Now, any other little surprises? Were you planning seismic surveys? I believe those usually involve explosives . . ."

A few hours later, the somewhat chastened scientist admitted that he had also found two bottles of elemental fluorine, used to power the lasers that could zap passing celestial bodies at thousand-kilometer ranges for spectrographic sampling. As pure fluorine was about the most vicious substance known to Man, it was high on the list of prohibited materials—but, like the rockets that drove the penetrometers down to their targets, it was essential for the mission.

When he was quite satisfied that all the necessary precautions had been taken, Captain Laplace accepted the scientist's apologies and his assurance

that the oversight was entirely due to the haste with which the expedition
had been organized.

He felt sure that Dr. Anderson was telling the truth, but already he felt
that there was something odd about the mission.

Just *how* odd he could never have imagined.

23 · Inferno

Before the detonation of Jupiter, Io had been second only to Venus as the best approximation to Hell in the Solar System. Now that Lucifer had raised its surface temperature another couple of hundred degrees, even Venus could no longer compete.

The sulfur volcanoes and geysers had multiplied their activity, now reshaping the features of the tormented satellite in years rather than decades. The planetologists had given up any attempt at map-making, and contented themselves with taking orbital photographs every few days. From these, they had constructed awe-inspiring time-lapse movies of Inferno in action.

Lloyds of London had charged a stiff premium for this leg of the mission, but Io posed no real danger to a ship doing a flyby at a minimum range of ten thousand kilometers—and over the relatively quiescent Night-side at that.

As he watched the approaching yellow and orange globe—the most improbably garish object in the entire Solar System—Second Officer Chris Floyd could not help recalling the time, now half a century ago, when his grandfather had come this way. Here *Leonov* had made its rendezvous with the abandoned *Discovery*, and here Dr. Chandra had reawakened the dormant computer HAL. Then both ships had flown on to survey the enormous black monolith hovering at L1, the Inner Lagrange Point between Io and Jupiter.

Now the monolith was gone—and so was Jupiter. The minisun that had risen like a phoenix from the implosion of the giant planet had turned its satellites into what was virtually another Solar System, though only on

Ganymede and Europa were there regions with Earthlike temperatures. How long that would continue to be the case, no one knew. Estimates of Lucifer's life-span ranged from a thousand to a million years.

Galaxy's science team looked wistfully at the L1 point, but it was now far too dangerous to approach. There had always been a river of electrical energy—the Io "flux tube"—flowing between Jupiter and its inner satellite, and the creation of Lucifer had increased its strength several hundredfold. Sometimes the river of power could even be seen by the naked eye, glowing yellow with the characteristic light of ionized sodium. Some engineers on Ganymede had talked about tapping the gigawatts going to waste next door, but no one could think of a plausible way of doing so.

The first penetrometer was launched, with vulgar comments from the crew, and two hours later drove like a hypodermic needle into the festering satellite. It continued to operate for almost five seconds—ten times its designed lifetime—broadcasting thousands of chemical, physical, and rheological measurements, before Io demolished it.

The scientists were ecstatic; van der Berg was merely pleased. He had expected the probe to work; Io was an absurdly easy target. But if he was right about Europa, the second penetrometer would surely fail.

Yet that would prove nothing; it might fail for a dozen good reasons. And when it did, there would be no alternative but a landing.

Which, of course, was totally prohibited—not only by the laws of Man.

24 · Shaka
the Great

ASTROPOL—which, despite its grandiose title, had disappointingly little business off-Earth—would not admit that Shaka really existed. The USSA took exactly the same position, and its diplomats became embarrassed or indignant when anyone was tactless enough to mention the name.

But Newton's Third Law applies in politics, as in everything else. The Bund had its extremists—though it tried, sometimes not very hard, to disown them—continually plotting against the USSA. Usually they confined themselves to attempts at commercial sabotage, but there were occasional explosions, disappearances, and even assassinations.

Needless to say, the South Africans did not take this lightly. They reacted by establishing their own official counterintelligence services, which also had a rather free-wheeling range of operations—and likewise claimed to know nothing about Shaka. Perhaps they were employing the useful CIA invention of "plausible deniability." It is even possible that they were telling the truth.

According to one theory, Shaka started as a codeword, and then—rather like Prokofiev's "Lieutenant Kije"—had acquired a life of its own, because it was useful to various clandestine bureaucracies. This would certainly account for the fact that none of its members had ever defected or even been arrested.

But there was another, somewhat farfetched explanation for this, according to those who believed that Shaka really did exist. All its agents had been psychologically conditioned to self-destruct before there was any possibility of interrogation.

Whatever the truth, no one could seriously imagine that, more than two centuries after his death, the legend of the great Zulu tyrant would cast its shadow across worlds he never knew.

25 · The Shrouded World

During the decade after the ignition of Jupiter and the spreading of the Great Thaw across its satellite system, Europa had been left strictly alone. Then the Chinese had made a swift flyby, probing the clouds with radar in an attempt to locate the wreck of the *Tsien*. They had been unsuccessful, but their maps of Dayside were the first to show the new continents now emerging as the ice cover melted.

They had also discovered a perfectly straight two-kilometer-long feature that looked so artificial that it was christened The Great Wall. Because of its shape and size it was assumed to be the monolith—or *a* monolith, since millions had been replicated in the hours before the creation of Lucifer.

However, there had been no reaction, or any hint of an intelligent signal, from below the steadily thickening clouds. So a few years later, survey satellites were placed in permanent orbit and high-altitude balloons were dropped into the atmosphere to study its wind patterns. Terrestrial meteorologists found these of absorbing interest, because Europa—with a central ocean and a sun that never set—presented a beautifully simplified model for their textbooks.

So had begun the game of "Europan Roulette," as the administrators were fond of calling it whenever the scientists proposed getting closer to the satellite. After fifty uneventful years, it had become somewhat boring. Captain Laplace hoped it would remain that way, and had required considerable reassurance from Dr. Anderson.

"Personally," he had told the scientist, "I would regard it as a slightly unfriendly act to have a ton of armor-piercing hardware dropped on me at

a thousand kilometers an hour. I'm quite surprised the World Council gave
you permission."

Dr. Anderson was also a little surprised, though he might not have been
had he known that the project was the last item on a long agenda of a
Science Subcommittee late on a Friday afternoon. Of such trifles History is
made.

"I agree, Captain. But we are operating under very strict limitations,
and there's no possibility of interfering with the—ah—Europans, whoever
they are. We're aiming at a target five kilometers above sea level."

"So I understand. What's so interesting about Mount Zeus?"

"It's a total mystery. It wasn't even *there* only a few years ago. So you
can understand why it drives the geologists crazy."

"And your gadget will analyze it when it goes in."

"Exactly. And—I really shouldn't be telling you this—but I've been
asked to keep the results confidential and to send them back to Earth
encrypted. Obviously, someone's on the track of a major discovery and
wants to make quite sure they're not beaten to publication. Would you
believe that scientists could be so petty?"

Captain Laplace could well believe it, but did not want to disillusion his
passenger. Dr. Anderson seemed touchingly naive; whatever was going on
—and the captain was now quite certain there was much more to this
mission than met the eye—Anderson knew nothing about it.

"I can only hope, Doctor, that the Europans don't go in for mountain
climbing. I'd hate to interrupt any attempt to put a flag on their local
Everest."

There was a feeling of unusual excitement aboard *Galaxy* when the penetrometer was launched—and even the inevitable jokes were muted. During
the two hours of the probe's long fall toward Europa, virtually every member of the crew found some perfectly legitimate excuse to visit the bridge
and watch the guidance operation. Fifteen minutes before impact, Captain
Laplace declared it out of bounds to all visitors, except the ship's new
steward Rosie; without her endless supply of squeezebulbs full of excellent
coffee, the operation could not have continued.

Everything went perfectly. Soon after atmospheric entry, the air brakes
were deployed, slowing the penetrometer to an acceptable impact velocity.
The radar image of the target—featureless, with no indication of scale—
grew steadily on the screen. At minus one second, all the recorders
switched automatically to high speed . . .

. . . But there was nothing to record. "Now I know," said Dr. Anderson sadly, "just how they felt at the Jet Propulsion Lab, when those first
Rangers crashed into the Moon—with their cameras blind."

26 · Night Watch

Only Time is universal; Night and Day are merely quaint local customs found on those planets that tidal forces have not yet robbed of their rotation. But however far they travel from their native world, human beings can never escape the diurnal rhythm, set ages ago by its cycle of light and darkness.

So at 0105, Universal Time, Second Officer Chang was alone on the bridge, while the ship was sleeping round him. There was no real need for him to be awake either, since *Galaxy*'s electronic sensors would detect any malfunction far sooner than he could possibly do. But a century of cybernetics had proved that human beings were still slightly better than machines at dealing with the unexpected; and sooner or later, the unexpected always happened.

Where's my coffee? thought Chang grumpily. It's not like Rosie to be late. He wondered if the steward had been affected by the same malaise that had overtaken both scientists and spacecrew after the disasters of the last twenty-four hours.

Following the failure of the first penetrometer, there had been a hasty conference to decide the next step. One unit was left; it had been intended for Callisto, but it could be used just as easily here.

"And anyway," Dr. Anderson had argued, "we've landed on Callisto—there's nothing there except assorted varieties of cracked ice."

There had been no disagreement. After a twelve-hour delay for modification and testing, penetrometer number 3 was launched into the Europan cloudscape, following the invisible track of its precursor.

This time, the ship's recorders *did* get some data—for about half a millisecond. The accelerometer on the probe, which was calibrated to operate up to 20,000 gee, gave one brief pulse before going off scale. Everything must have been destroyed in very much less than the twinkling of an eye.

After a second, and even gloomier, postmortem, it was decided to report to Earth and wait in high orbit round Europa for any further instructions before proceeding to Callisto and the outer moons.

"Sorry to be late, sir," said Rose McCullen (one would never guess from her name that she was slightly darker than the coffee she was carrying), "but I must have set the alarm wrong."

"Lucky for us," the officer of the watch said with a chuckle, "that *you're* not running the ship."

"I don't understand how *anyone* could run it," answered Rose. "It all looks so complicated."

"Oh, it's not as bad as it looks," said Chang. "And don't they give you basic space theory in your training course?"

"Er—yes. But I never understood much of it. Orbits and all that nonsense."

Second Officer Chang was bored, and felt it would be a kindness to enlighten his audience. And although Rose was not exactly his type, she was undoubtedly attractive; a little effort now might be a worthwhile investment. It never occurred to him that, having performed her duty, Rose might like to go back to sleep.

Twenty minutes later, Second Officer Chang waved at the navigation console and concluded expansively: "So you see, it's really almost automatic. You only have to punch in a few numbers and the ship takes care of the rest."

Rose seemed to be getting tired; she kept looking at her watch.

"I'm sorry," said the suddenly contrite Chang. "I shouldn't have kept you up."

"Oh no—it's extremely interesting. Please go on."

"Definitely not. Maybe some other time. Good night, Rosie—and thanks for the coffee."

"Good night, sir."

Steward Third Class Rose McCullen glided (not too skillfully) toward the still-open door. Chang did not bother to look back when he heard it close.

It was thus a considerable shock when, a few seconds later, he was addressed by a completely unfamiliar female voice.

"Mr. Chang—don't bother to touch the alarm button—it's disconnected. Here are the landing coordinates. Take the ship down."

Slowly, wondering if he had somehow dozed off and was having a nightmare, Chang rotated his chair.

The person who had been Rose McCullen was floating beside the oval hatchway, steadying herself by holding on to the locking lever of the door. Everything about her seemed to have changed; in a moment of time, their roles had been reversed. The shy steward—who had never before looked at him directly—was now regarding Chang with a cold, merciless stare that made him feel like a rabbit hypnotized by a snake. The small but deadly looking gun nestling in her free hand seemed an unnecessary adornment; Chang had not the slighest doubt that she could very efficiently kill him without it.

Nevertheless, both his self-respect and his professional honor demanded that he should not surrender without some sort of a struggle. At the very least, he might be able to gain time.

"Rose," he said—and now his lips had difficulty in forming a name that had suddenly become inappropriate—"this is perfectly ridiculous. What I told you just now—it's simply not true. I couldn't possibly land the ship by myself. It would take hours to compute the correct orbit, and I'd need someone to help me. A copilot, at least."

The gun did not waver.

"I'm not a fool, Mr. Chang. This ship isn't energy-limited, like the old chemical rockets. The escape velocity of Europa is only three kilometers a second. Part of your training is an emergency landing with the main computer down. Now you can put it into practice: the window for an optimum touchdown at the coordinates I gave you opens in five minutes."

"That type of abort," said Chang, now beginning to sweat profusely, "has an estimated twenty-five percent failure rate"—the true figure was ten percent, but in the circumstances he felt that a little exaggeration was justified—"and it's years since I checked out on it."

"In that case," answered Rose McCullen, "I'll have to eliminate you and ask the captain to send me someone more qualified. Annoying, because we'll miss this window and have to wait a couple of hours for the next one. Four minutes left."

Second Officer Chang knew when he was beaten; but at least he had tried.

"Let me have those coordinates," he said.

27 · Rosie

Captain Laplace woke instantly at the first gentle tapping, like a distant woodpecker, of the attitude control jets. For a moment he wondered if he was dreaming: no, the ship was definitely turning in space.

Perhaps it was getting too hot on one side and the thermal control system was making some minor adjustments. That did happen occasionally, and was a black mark for the officer on duty, who should have noticed that the temperature envelope was being approached.

He reached for the intercom button to call—who was it?—Mr. Chang on the bridge. His hand never completed the movement.

After days of weightlessness, even a tenth of a gravity is a shock. To the captain it seemed like minutes, though it must have been only a few seconds, before he could unbuckle his restraining harness and struggle out of his bunk. This time, he found the button and jabbed it viciously. There was no reply.

He tried to ignore the thuds and bumps of inadequately secured objects that had been taken unawares by the onset of gravity. Things seemed to go on falling for a long time, but presently the only abnormal sound was the muffled, far-off scream of the drive at full blast.

He tore open the curtain of the cabin's little window and looked out at the stars. He knew roughly where the ship's axis *should* have been pointing; even if he could only judge it to within thirty or forty degrees, that would allow him to distinguish between the two possible alternatives.

Galaxy could be vectored either to gain, or to lose, orbital velocity. It was losing it—and therefore preparing to fall toward Europa.

There was an insistent banging on the door, and the captain realized that little more than a minute could really have passed. Second Officer Floyd and two other crew members were crowded in the narrowing passageway.

"The bridge is locked, sir," Floyd reported breathlessly. "We can't get in —and Chang doesn't answer. We don't know what's happened."

"I'm afraid I do," Captain Laplace answered, climbing into his shorts. "Some madman was bound to try it sooner or later. We've been hijacked, and I know to where. But I'm damned if I know *why*."

He glanced at his watch and did a quick mental calculation.

"At this thrust level, we'll have deorbited within fifteen minutes—make it ten for safety. Anyway, can we cut the drive without endangering the ship?"

Second Officer Yu, Engineering, looked very unhappy but volunteered a reluctant reply.

"We could pull the circuit breakers in the pump motor lines and cut off the propellant supply."

"Can we get at them?"

"Yes—they're on Deck Three."

"Then let's go."

"Er—then the independent backup system would take over. For safety, that's behind a sealed bulkhead on Deck Five—we'd have to get a cutter— no, it couldn't be done in time."

Captain Laplace had been afraid of that. The men of genius who had designed *Galaxy* had tried to protect the ship from all plausible accidents. There was no way they could have safeguarded it against human malevolence.

"Any alternatives?"

"Not in the time available. I'm afraid."

"Then let's get to the bridge and see if we can talk to Chang—and whoever is with him."

And who could that be? he wondered. He refused to believe that it could be one of his regular crew. That left—of course, there was the answer! He could see it all. Monomaniac researcher tries to prove theory; experiments frustrated; decides that the quest for knowledge takes precedence over everything else . . .

It was uncomfortably like one of those cheap mad-scientist melodramas, but it fit the facts perfectly. He wondered if Dr. Anderson had decided that this was the only road to a Nobel prize.

That theory was swiftly demolished when the breathless and disheveled geologist arrived, gasping. "For God's sake, Captain—what's happening? We're under full thrust! Are we going up—or down?"

"Down," answered Captain Laplace. "In about ten minutes we'll be in an orbit that will hit Europa. I can only hope that whoever's at the control knows what he's doing."

Now they were at the bridge, facing the closed door. Not a sound came from the far side.

Laplace rapped as loudly as he possibly could without bruising his knuckles.

"This is the captain! Let us in!"

He felt rather foolish at giving an order that would certainly be ignored, but he hoped for at least some reaction. To his surprise, he got one.

The external speaker hissed into life, and a voice said: "Don't attempt anything foolish, Captain. I have a gun, and Mr. Chang is obeying my orders."

"Who was *that*?" whispered one of the officers. "It sounds like a woman!"

"You're right," said the captain grimly. That certainly cut down the alternatives, but didn't help matters in any way.

"What do you hope to *do*? You know you can't possibly get away with it!" he shouted, trying to sound masterful rather than plaintive.

"We're landing on Europa. And if you want to take off again, don't try to stop me."

"Her room's completely clean," Second Officer Chris Floyd reported thirty minutes later, when the thrust had been cut to zero and *Galaxy* was falling along the ellipse that would soon graze the atmosphere of Europa. They were committed; although it would now be possible to immobilize the engines, it would be suicide to do so. They would be needed again to make a landing—although that could be merely a more protracted form of suicide.

"Rosie McCullen! Who would have believed it! Do you suppose she's on drugs?"

"No," said Floyd. "This has been very carefully planned. She must have a radio hidden *somewhere* in the ship. We should search for it."

"You sound like a damned cop."

"That will do, gentlemen," said the captain. Tempers were getting frayed, largely through sheer frustration and the total failure to establish any further contact with the barricaded bridge. He glanced at his watch.

"Less than two hours before we enter atmosphere—what there is of it. I'll be in my cabin—it's just possible they may try to call me there. Mr. Yu, please stand by the bridge and report any developments at once."

He had never felt so helpless in his life, but there were times when doing nothing was the only thing to do. As he left the officer's wardroom, he heard someone say wistfully: "I could do with a bulb of coffee. Rosie made the best I've ever tasted."

Yes, thought the captain grimly, she's certainly efficient. *Whatever* job she tackles, she'll do it thoroughly.

28 · Dialog

There was only one man aboard *Galaxy* who could regard the situation as anything but a total disaster. I may be about to die, Rolf van der Berg told himself; but at least I have a chance of scientific immortality. Though that might be poor consolation, it was more than anyone else on the ship could hope for.

That *Galaxy* was heading for Mount Zeus he did not doubt for a moment; there was nothing else on Europa of any significance. Indeed, there was nothing remotely comparable on *any* planet.

So his theory—and he had to admit that it was still a theory—was no longer a secret. How could it have leaked out?

He trusted Uncle Paul implicitly, but he might have been indiscreet. More likely someone had monitored his computers, perhaps as a matter of routine. If so, the old scientist could well be in danger; Rolf wondered if he could—or should—get a warning to him. He knew that the communications officer was trying to contact Ganymede via one of the emergency transmitters; an automatic beacon alert had already gone out, and the news would be hitting Earth any minute now. It had been on its way now for almost an hour.

"Come in," he said, at the quiet knock on his cabin door. "Oh—hello, Chris. What can I do for you?"

He was surprised to see Second Officer Chris Floyd, whom he knew no better than any of his other colleagues. If they landed safely on Europa, he thought gloomily, they might get to know each other far better than they wished.

"Hello, Doctor. You're the only person who lives around here. I wondered if you could help me."

"I'm not sure how anyone can help anyone at the moment. What's the latest from the bridge?"

"Nothing new. I've just left Yu and Gillings up there, trying to fix a mike on the door. But no one inside seems to be talking; not surprising—Chang must have his hands full."

"Can he get us down safely?"

"He's the best; if anyone can do it, *he* can. I'm more worried about getting off again."

"God—I'd not been looking that far ahead. I assumed that was no problem."

"It could be marginal. Remember, this ship is designed for orbital operations. We hadn't planned to put down on *any* major moon—though we hoped to rendezvous with Ananke and Carme. So we could be stuck on Europa—especially if Chang has to waste propellant looking for a good landing site."

"Do we know where he *is* trying to land?" Rolf asked, attempting not to sound more interested than might be reasonably expected. He must have failed, because Chris looked at him sharply.

"There's no way we can tell at this stage, though we may get a better idea when he starts braking. But you know these moons; where do *you* think?"

"There's only one interesting place. Mount Zeus."

"Why should anyone want to land there?"

Rolf shrugged. "That was one of the things we'd hoped to find out. Cost us two expensive penetrometers."

"And it looks like costing a great deal more. Haven't you *any* ideas?"

"You sound like a cop," said van der Berg with a grin, not intending it in the least seriously.

"Funny—that's the second time I've been told that in the last hour."

Instantly, there was a subtle change in the atmosphere of the cabin—almost as if the life-support system had readjusted itself.

"Oh—I was just joking—*are* you?"

"If I was, I wouldn't admit it, would I?"

That was no answer, thought van der Berg; but on second thought, perhaps it was.

He looked intently at the young officer, noticing—not for the first time—his striking resemblance to his famous grandfather. Someone had mentioned that Chris Floyd had only joined *Galaxy* on this mission, from another ship in the Tsung fleet—adding sarcastically that it was useful to have good connections in any business. But there had been no criticism of Floyd's ability; he was an excellent space officer. Those skills might qualify him for other part-time jobs, as well; look at Rosie McMahon—who had also, now he came to think of it, joined *Galaxy* just before this mission.

Rolf van der Berg felt he had become enmeshed in some vast and tenuous web of interplanetary intrigue; as a scientist, accustomed to getting—usually—straightforward answers to the questions he put to Nature, he did not enjoy the situation.

But he could hardly claim to be an innocent victim. He had tried to conceal the truth—or at least what he believed to be the truth. And now the consequences of that deceit had multiplied like the neutrons in a chain reaction, with results that might be equally disastrous.

Which side was Chris Floyd on? How many sides *were* there? The Bund would certainly be involved, once the secret had leaked out. But there were splinter groups within the Bund itself, and groups opposing them; it was like a hall of mirrors.

There was one point, however, on which he did feel reasonably certain. Chris Floyd, if only because of his connections, could be trusted. I'd put my money, thought van der Berg, on his being assigned to ASTROPOL for the duration of the mission—however long, or short, *that* might now be . . .

"I'd like to help you, Chris," he said slowly. "As you probably suspect, I do have some theories. But they may still be utter nonsense—

"In less than half an hour, we may know the truth. Until then, I prefer to say nothing."

And this is not, he told himself, merely ingrained Boer stubbornness. If he had been mistaken, he would prefer not to die among men who knew that *he* was the fool who had brought them to their doom.

29 · Descent

Second Officer Chang had been wrestling with the problem ever since *Galaxy* had been successfully—to his surprise as much as his relief—injected into transfer orbit. For the next couple of hours she was in the hands of God, or at least Sir Isaac Newton; there was nothing to do but wait until the final braking and descent maneuver.

He had briefly considered trying to fool Rose by giving the ship a reverse vector at closest approach, and so taking it out into space again. It would then be back in a stable orbit, and a rescue could eventually be mounted from Ganymede. But there was a fundamental objection to this scheme: *he* would certainly not be alive to be rescued. Though Chang was no coward, he would prefer not to become a posthumous hero of the spaceways.

It any event, his chances of surviving the next hour seemed remote. He had been ordered to take down, *single-handed*, a three thousand tonner on totally unknown territory. This was not a feat he would care to attempt even on the familiar Moon.

"How many minutes before you start braking?" asked Rosie. Perhaps it was more of an order than a question; she clearly understood the fundamentals of astronautics, and Chang abandoned his last wild fantasies of outwitting her.

"Five," he said reluctantly. "Can I warn the rest of the ship to stand by?"

"I'll do it. Give me the mike . . . THIS IS THE BRIDGE. WE START BRAKING IN FIVE MINUTES. REPEAT, FIVE MINUTES. OUT."

To the scientists and officers assembled in the wardroom, the message was fully expected. They had had one piece of luck; the external video monitors had not been switched off. Perhaps Rose had forgotten about them; it was more likely that she had not bothered. So now, as helpless spectators—quite literally, a captive audience—they could watch their unfolding doom.

The cloudy crescent of Europa now filled the field of the rear-view camera. There was no break anywhere in the solid overcast of water vapor recondensing on its way back to Nightside. That was not important, since the landing would be radar controlled until the last moment. It would, however, prolong the agony of observers who had to rely on visible light.

No one stared more intently at the approaching world than the man who had studied it with such frustration for almost a decade. Rolf van der Berg, seated in one of the flimsy low-gravity chairs with the restraining belt lightly fastened, barely noticed the first onset of weight as braking commenced.

In five seconds, they were up to full thrust. All the officers were doing rapid calculations on their comsets; without access to Navigation, there would be a lot of guesswork, and Captain Laplace waited for a consensus to emerge.

"Eleven minutes," he announced presently, "assuming he doesn't reduce thrust level—he's at max now. And assuming he's going to hover at ten kilometers—just above the overcast—and then go straight down. That could take another five minutes."

It was unnecessary for him to add that the last second of those five minutes would be the most critical.

Europa seemed determined to keep its secrets to the very end. When *Galaxy* was hovering motionless, just above the cloudscape, there was still no sign of the land—or sea—beneath. Then, for a few agonizing seconds, the screens became completely blank—except for a glimpse of the now-extended, and very seldom used, landing gear. The noise of its emergence a few minutes earlier had caused a brief flurry of alarm among the passengers; now they could only hope that it would perform its duty.

How thick is this damn cloud? van der Berg asked himself. Does it go all the way down—

No, it was breaking, thinning out into sheds and wisps—and there was the New Europa, spread out, it seemed, only a few thousand meters below.

It was indeed new; one did not have to be a geologist to see that. Four billion years ago, perhaps, the infant Earth had looked like this, as land and sea prepared to begin their endless conflict.

Here, until fifty years ago, there had been neither land nor sea—only ice. But now the ice had melted on the Lucifer-facing hemisphere, the resulting water had boiled upward—and been deposited in the permanent deep freeze of Nightside. The removal of billions of tons of liquid from one hemisphere to the other had thus exposed ancient seabeds that had never before known even the pale light of the far-distant sun.

Someday, perhaps, these contorted landscapes would be softened and tamed by a spreading blanket of vegetation; now they were barren lava flows and gently steaming mud flats, interrupted occasionally by masses of upthrust rock with strangely slanting strata. This had clearly been an area of great tectonic disturbance, which was hardly surprising if it had seen the recent birth of a mountain the size of Everest.

And there it was—looming up over the unnaturally close horizon. Rolf van der Berg felt a tightness in his chest and a tingling of the flesh at the back of his neck. No longer through the remote impersonal senses of instruments, but with his own eyes, he was seeing the mountain of his dreams.

As he well knew, it was in the approximate shape of a tetrahedron, tilted so that one face was almost vertical. (*That* would be a nice challenge to climbers, even in this gravity—especially as they couldn't drive pitons into it . . .) The summit was hidden in the clouds, and much of the gently sloping face turned toward them was covered with snow.

"Is *that* what all the fuss is about?" muttered someone in disgust. "Looks like a perfectly ordinary mountain to me. I guess that once you've seen one—" He was *shushed* angrily into silence.

Galaxy was now drifting slowly toward Mount Zeus, as Chang searched for a good landing place. The ship had very little lateral control, as ninety percent of the main thrust had to be used merely to support it. There was enough propellant to hover for perhaps five minutes; after that, he might still be able to land safely—but he could never take off again.

Neil Armstrong had faced the same dilemma, almost a hundred years ago. But he had not been piloting with a gun aimed at his head.

Yet for the last few minutes, Chang had totally forgotten both gun and Rosie. Every sense was focused on the job ahead; he was virtually part of the great machine he was controlling. The only human emotion left to him was not fear but exhilaration. This was the job he had been trained to perform; *this* was the highlight of his professional career—even as it might be the finale.

And that was what it looked like it was becoming. The foot of the mountain was now less than a kilometer away—and he had still found no landing site. The terrain was incredibly rugged, torn with canyons, littered with gigantic boulders. He had not seen a single horizontal area larger than a tennis court—and the red line on the propellant gauge was only thirty seconds away.

But *there*, at last, was a smooth surface—much the flattest he'd seen. It was his only chance within the time frame.

Delicately he juggled the giant, unstable cylinder toward the patch of horizontal ground—it seemed to be snow-covered—yes, it was—the blast was blowing the snow away—but what's underneath?—looks like ice—must be a frozen lake—how thick—HOW THICK—

The five hundred–ton hammer-blow of *Galaxy*'s main jets hit the treacherously inviting surface. A pattern of radiating lines spread swiftly across it; the ice cracked, and great sheets started to overturn. Concentric waves of boiling water hurtled outward as the fury of the drive blasted into the suddenly uncovered lake.

Like the well-trained officer he was, Chang reacted automatically, without the fatal hesitations of thought. His left hand ripped open the safety lock bar; his right grabbed the red lever it protected and pulled it to the open position.

The ABORT program, peacefully sleeping ever since *Galaxy* was launched, took over and hurled the ship back up into the sky.

30 · *Galaxy*
Down

In the wardroom, the sudden surge of full thrust came like a stay of execution. The horrified officers had seen the collapse of the chosen landing site and knew that there was only one way of escape. Now that Chang had taken it, they once more permitted themselves the luxury of breath.

But how long they could continue to enjoy that experience, no one could guess. Only Chang knew whether the ship had enough propellant to reach a stable orbit; and even if it did, Captain Laplace thought gloomily, the lunatic with the gun might order him down again. Though he did not for a minute believe that she really was a lunatic; she knew exactly what she was doing.

Suddenly there was a change in thrust.

"Number four motor's just cut," said an engineering officer. "I'm not surprised—probably overheated. Not rated for so long at this level."

There was, of course, no sense of any directional change—the reduced thrust was still along the ship's axis—but the views on the monitor screens had tilted crazily. *Galaxy* was still ascending, but no longer vertically. She had become a ballistic missile, aimed at some unknown target on Europa.

Once more, the thrust dropped abruptly; across the video monitors, the horizon became level again.

"He's cut the opposite motor—only way to stop us cartwheeling—but can he maintain altitude? Good man!"

The watching scientists could not see what was good about it; the view on the monitors had disappeared completely, obscured by a blinding white fog.

"He's dumping excess propellant—lightening the ship—"

The thrust dwindled away to zero; the ship was in free fall. In a few seconds, it had dropped through the vast cloud of ice crystals created when its dumped propellant had exploded into space. And there beneath it, approaching at a leisurely one-eighth of a gravity acceleration, was Europa's central sea. At least Chang would not have to select a landing site; from now on, it would be standard operating procedure, familiar as a video game to millions who had never gone into space and never would.

All you had to do was to balance the thrust against gravity, so that the descending ship reached zero velocity at zero altitude. There was some margin for error, but not much, even for the water landings that the first American astronauts had preferred and that Chang was now reluctantly emulating. If he made a mistake—and after the last few hours, he could scarcely be blamed—no home computer would say to him: "Sorry—you've crashed. Would you like to try again? Answer YES/NO . . ."

Second Officer Yu and his two companions, waiting with their improvised weapons outside the locked door of the bridge, had perhaps been given the toughest assignment of all. They had no monitor screens to tell them what was happening, and had to rely on messages from the wardroom. Nor had there been anything through the spy mike, which was hardly surprising. Chang and McMahon had very little time or need for conversation.

The touchdown was superb, with hardly a jolt. *Galaxy* sank a few extra meters, then bobbed up again, to float vertically and—thanks to the weight of the engines—in the upright position.

It was then that the listeners heard the first intelligible sounds through the spy mike.

"You maniac, Rosie," said Chang's voice, more in resigned exhaustion than anger. "I hope you're satisfied. You've killed us all."

There was one pistol shot, then a long silence.

Yu and his colleagues waited patiently, knowing that something was bound to happen soon. Then they heard the locking levers being unlatched and gripped the spanners and metal bars they were carrying. She might get one of them, but not all.

The door swung open, very slowly.

"Sorry," said Second Officer Chang. "I must have passed out for a minute."

Then, like any reasonable man, he fainted again.

31 · The Sea
of Galilee

I can never understand how a man could become a doctor, Captain
Laplace told himself. Or an undertaker, for that matter. They have some
nasty jobs to do . . .

"Well, did you find anything?"

"No, Skipper. Of course, I don't have the right sort of equipment. There
are some implants that you could only locate through a microscope—or so
I'm told. They could only be very short range, though."

"Perhaps to a relay transmitter somewhere in the ship—Floyd's suggested we make a search. You took fingerprints and—any other idents?"

"Yes—when we contact Ganymede, we'll beam them up, with her papers. But I doubt if we'll ever know who Rosie was, or who she was acting
for. Or *why*, for God's sake."

"At least she showed some human instincts," said Laplace thoughtfully.
"She must have known she'd failed when Chang pulled the abort lever.
She could have shot him then instead of letting him land."

"Much good *that* will do us, I'm afraid. Let me tell you something that
happened when Jenkins and I put the cadaver out through the refuse
dump."

The doctor pursed his lips in a grimace of distaste.

"You were right, of course—it was the only thing to do. Well, we didn't
bother to attach any weights; it floated for a few minutes. We watched to
see if it would clear the ship, and then—"

The doctor seemed to be struggling for words.

"What, dammit?"

"*Something* came up out of the water. Like a parrot beak, but about a hundred times bigger. It took—Rosie—with one snap, and disappeared. We have some impressive company here; even if we could breathe outside, I certainly wouldn't recommend swimming—"

"Bridge to Captain," said the officer on duty. "Big disturbance in the water. Camera three—I'll give you the picture."

"That's the thing I saw!" cried the doctor. He felt a sudden chill at the inevitable, ominous thought: *I hope it's not back for more.*

Suddenly a vast bulk broke through the surface of the ocean and arched into the sky. For a moment, the whole monstrous shape was suspended between air and water.

The familiar can be as shocking as the strange—when it is in the wrong place. Both captain and doctor exclaimed simultaneously: "It's a shark!"

There was just time to notice a few subtle differences—in addition to the monstrous parrot-beak—before the giant crashed back into the sea. There was an extra pair of fins—and there appeared to be no gills. Nor were there any eyes, but on either side of the beak there were curious protuberances that might be some other sense organs.

"Convergent evolution, of course," said the doctor. "Same problems— same solutions, on any planet. Look at Earth. Sharks, dolphins, ichthyosaurs—all oceanic predators must have the same basic design. That beak puzzles me, though—"

"What's it doing now?"

The creature had surfaced again, but now it was moving very slowly, as if exhausted after that one gigantic leap. In fact, it seemed to be in trouble —even in agony; it was beating its tail against the sea, without attempting to move in any definite direction.

Suddenly it vomited its last meal, turned belly up, and lay wallowing lifelessly in the gentle swell.

"Oh, my God," whispered the captain, his voice full of revulsion. "I think I know what's happened."

"Totally alien biochemistries," said the doctor; even he seemed shaken by the sight. "Rosie's claimed one victim, after all."

The Sea of Galilee was, of course, named after the man who had discovered Europa—as he in turn had been named after a much smaller sea on another world.

It was a very young sea, being less than fifty years old; and like most newborn infants, it could be quite boisterous. Although the Europan atmosphere was still too thin to generate real hurricanes, a steady wind blew from the surrounding land toward the tropical zone at the point above which Lucifer was stationary. Here, at the point of perpetual noon, the water was continually boiling—though at a temperature, in this thin atmosphere, barely hot enough to make a good cup of tea.

Luckily, the steamy, turbulent region immediately beneath Lucifer was a thousand kilometers away; *Galaxy* had descended in a relatively calm area, less than a hundred kilometers from the nearest land. At peak velocity, she could cover that distance in a fraction of a second; but now, as she drifted beneath the low-hanging clouds of Europa's permanent overcast, land seemed as far-off as the remotest quasar. To make matters worse—if possible—the eternal off-shore wind was taking her farther out to sea. And even if she could manage to ground herself on some virgin beach of this new world, she might be no better off than she was now.

But she would be more comfortable; spaceships, though admirably watertight, are seldom seaworthy. *Galaxy* was floating in a vertical position, bobbing up and down with gentle but disturbing oscillations; half the crew was already sick.

Captain Laplace's first action, after he had been through the damage reports, was to appeal for anyone with experience in handling boats—of any size or shape. It seemed reasonable to suppose that among thirty astronautical engineers and space scientists there should be a considerable amount of seafaring talent, and he immediately located five amateur sailors and even one professional—Purser Frank Lee, who had started his career with the Tsung shipping lines and then switched to space.

Although pursers were more accustomed to handling accounting machines (often, in Frank Lee's case, a two-hundred-year-old ivory abacus) than navigational instruments, they still had to pass exams in basic seamanship. Lee had never had a chance of testing his maritime skills; now, almost a billion kilometers from the South China Sea, his time had come.

"We should flood the propellant tanks," he told the captain. "Then we'll ride lower and won't be bobbing up and down so badly."

It seemed foolish to let even more water into the ship, and the captain hesitated.

"Suppose we run aground?"

No one made the obvious comment "What difference will it make?" Without any serious discussion, it had been assumed that they would be better off on land—if they could ever reach it.

"We can always blow the tanks again. We'll have to do that anyway, when we reach shore, to get the ship into a horizontal position. Thank God we have power . . ."

His voice trailed off; everyone knew what he meant. Without the auxiliary reactor that was running the life-support systems, they would all be dead within hours. Now—barring a breakdown—the ship could sustain them indefinitely.

Ultimately, of course, they would starve; they had just had dramatic proof that there was no nourishment, but only poison, in the seas of Europa.

   At least they had made contact with Ganymede, so that the entire human race now knew their predicament. The best brains in the Solar System would now be trying to save them. If they failed, the passengers and crew of *Galaxy* would have the consolation of dying in the full glare of publicity.

IV
At
the
Water
Hole

32 · Diversion

"The latest news," said Captain Smith to his assembled passengers, "is that *Galaxy* is afloat, and in fairly good condition. One crew member—a woman steward—has been killed. We don't know the details. But everyone else is safe.

"The ship's systems are all working; there are a few leaks, but they've been controlled. Captain Laplace says there's no immediate danger, but the prevailing wind is driving them farther away from the mainland, toward the center of Dayside. That's not a serious problem—there are several large islands they're virtually certain to reach first. At the moment they're ninety kilometers from the nearest land. They've seen some large marine animals, but they show no sign of hostility.

"Barring further accidents, they should be able to survive for several months, until they run out of food—which of course is now being strictly rationed. But according to Captain Laplace, morale is still high.

"Now, this is where we come in. If we return to Earth immediately, get refueled and refitted, we can reach Europa in a retrograde-powered orbit in eighty-five days. *Universe* is the only ship currently commissioned that can land there *and* take off again with a reasonable payload. The Ganymede shuttles may be able to drop supplies, but that's all—though it may make the difference between life and death.

"I'm sorry, ladies and gentlemen, that our visit has been cut short—but I think you'll agree that we've shown you everything we promised. And I'm sure you'll approve of our new mission—even though the chances of success are, frankly, rather slim. That's all for the moment. Dr. Floyd—can I have a word with you?"

As the others drifted slowly and thoughtfully from the main lounge—scene of so many less portentous briefings—the captain scanned a clipboard full of messages. There were still occasions when words printed on pieces of paper were the most convenient medium of communication, but even here technology had made its mark. The sheets that the captain was reading were made of the indefinitely reusable multifax material that had done so much to reduce the load on the humble wastepaper basket.

"Heywood," he said—now that the formalities were over, "as you can guess, the circuits are burning up. And there's a lot going on that I don't understand."

"Ditto," answered Floyd. "Anything from Chris yet?"

"No, but Ganymede's relayed your message; he should have had it by now. There's a priority override on private communications, as you can imagine—but of course your name overrode *that*."

"Thanks, Skipper. Anything I can do to help?"

"Not really—I'll let you know."

It was almost the last time, for quite a while, that they would be on speaking terms with each other. Within a few hours Dr. Heywood Floyd would become "That crazy old fool!" and the short-lived "Mutiny on the *Universe*" would have begun—led by the captain.

It was not actually Heywood Floyd's idea; he only wished it was . . .

Second Officer Roy Jolson was "Stars," the navigation officer; Floyd barely knew him by sight, and had never had occasion to say more than "Good morning" to him. Floyd was quite surprised, therefore, by the navigator's diffident knock on his cabin door.

The astrogator was carrying a set of charts and seemed a little ill at ease. He could not be overawed by Floyd's presence—everyone on board now took him for granted—so there must be some other reason.

"Dr. Floyd," he began, in a tone of such urgent anxiety that he reminded his listener of a salesman whose entire future depends on making the next deal. "I'd like your advice—and assistance."

"Of course—but what can I do?"

Jolson unrolled the chart showing the position of all the planets inside the orbit of Lucifer.

"Your old trick of coupling *Leonov* and *Discovery*, to escape from Jupiter before it blew up, gave me the idea."

"It wasn't mine. Walter Curnow thought of it."

"Oh—I never knew that. Of course, we don't have another ship to boost us here—but we have something much better."

"What do you mean?" asked Floyd, completely baffled.

"Don't laugh. Why go back to Earth to take on propellant—when Old Faithful is blasting out tons every second, a couple of hundred meters away? If we tapped that, we could get to Europa not in three months but in three *weeks*."

The concept was so obvious, yet so daring, that it took Floyd's breath away. He could see half a dozen objections instantly; but none of them seemed fatal.

"What does the captain think of the idea?"

"I've not told him; that's why I need your help. I'd like you to check my calculations—then put the idea to him. He'd turn me down—I'm quite certain—and I don't blame him. If *I* was captain, I think I would too . . ."

There was a long silence in the little cabin. Then Heywood Floyd said slowly: "Let me give you all the reasons why it can't be done. Then you can tell me why I'm wrong."

Second Officer Jolson knew his commander; Captain Smith had never heard such a crazy suggestion in his life . . .

His objections were all well founded and showed little, if any trace of the notorious "Not Invented Here" syndrome.

"Oh, it would work in *theory*," he admitted. "But think of the practical problems, man! How would you get the stuff into the tanks?"

"I've talked to the engineers. We'd move the ship to the edge of the crater—it's quite safe to get within fifty meters. There's plumbing in the unfurnished section we can rip out—then we'd run a line to Old Faithful and wait until he spouts; you know how reliable and well behaved he is."

"But our pumps can't operate in a near vacuum!"

"We don't need them; we can rely on the geyser's own efflux velocity to give us an input of at least a hundred kilos a second. Old Faithful will do all the work."

"He'll just give ice crystals and steam, not liquid water."

"It will condense when it gets onboard."

"You've really thought this out, haven't you?" said the captain with grudging admiration. "But I just don't believe it. Is the water pure enough, for one thing? What about contaminants—especially carbon particles?"

Floyd could not help smiling. Captain Smith was developing an obsession about soot.

"We can filter out large ones; the rest won't affect the reaction. Oh yes—the hydrogen isotope ratio here looks *better* than for Earth. You may even get some extra thrust."

"What do your colleagues think of the idea? If we head straight for Lucifer, it may be months before they can get home—"

"I've not spoken to them. But does it matter when so many lives are at stake? We may reach *Galaxy* seventy days ahead of schedule! *Seventy days*! Think what could happen on Europa in that time!"

"I'm perfectly aware of the time factor," snapped the captain. "That applies to us, as well. We may not have provisions for such an extended trip."

Now he's straining at gnats, thought Floyd, and he must know that I know it. Better be tactful . . .

"An extra couple of weeks? I can't believe we have so narrow a margin. You've been feeding us too well, anyway. Do some of us good to be on short rations for a while."

The captain managed a frosty smile. "You can tell that to Willis and Mihailovich. But I'm afraid the whole idea is insane."

"At least let us try it on the owners. I'd like to speak to Sir Lawrence."

"I can't stop you, of course," said Captain Smith, in a tone that suggested he wished he could. "But I know exactly what he'll say."

He was quite wrong.

Sir Lawrence Tsung had not placed a bet for thirty years; it was no longer in keeping with his august position in the world of commerce. But as a young man he had often enjoyed a mild flutter at the Hong Kong Race Course, before a puritanical administration had closed it in a fit of public morality. It was typical of life, Sir Lawrence sometimes thought wistfully, that when he could bet he had no money—and now he couldn't, because the richest man in the world had to set a good example.

And yet, as nobody knew better than he did, his whole business career had been one long gamble. He had done his utmost to control the odds by gathering the best information and listening to the experts his hunches told him would give the wisest advice. He had usually pulled out in time when they were wrong; but there had always been an element of risk.

Now, as he read the memorandum from Heywood Floyd, he felt again the old thrill he had not known since he had watched the horses thundering round into the last lap. Here was a gamble indeed—perhaps the last and greatest of his career—though he would never dare tell his Board of Directors. Still less the Lady Jasmine.

"Bill," he said, "what do you think?"

His son (steady and reliable, but lacking that vital spark that was perhaps no longer needed in this generation) gave him the answer he expected.

"The theory is quite sound. *Universe* can do it—on paper. But we've lost one ship. We'll be risking another."

"She's going to Jupiter—Lucifer—anyway."

"Yes—but after a complete checkout in Earth orbit. And do you realize what this proposed direct mission will involve? She'll be smashing all speed records—doing over a thousand kilometers a second at Turnaround!"

It was the worse thing he could possibly have said; once again the thunder of hooves sounded in his father's ears.

But Sir Lawrence merely answered: "It won't do any harm for them to make some tests, though Captain Smith is fighting the idea tooth and nail. Even threatens to resign. Meanwhile, just check the position with Lloyds —we may have to back down on the *Galaxy* claim."

Especially, he might have added, if we're going to throw *Universe* on to the table as an even bigger chip.

And he was worried about Captain Smith. Now that Laplace was stranded on Europa, Smith was the best commander he had left.

33 · Pit Stop

"Sloppiest job I've seen since I left college," grumbled the chief engineer. "But it's the best we can do in the time."

The makeshift pipeline stretched across fifty meters of dazzling, chemical-encrusted rock to the now quiescent vent of Old Faithful, where it ended in a rectangular, downward-pointing funnel. The Sun had just risen over the hills, and already the ground had begun to tremble slightly as the geyser's subterranean—or subhallean—reservoirs felt the first touch of warmth.

Watching from the observation lounge, Heywood Floyd could hardly believe that so much had happened in a mere twenty-four hours. First of all, the ship had split into two rival factions—one led by the captain, the other perforce headed by himself. They had been coldly polite to each other, and there had been no actual exchange of blows: but he had discovered that in certain quarters he now rejoiced in the nickname of "Suicide Floyd." It was not an honor that he particularly appreciated.

Yet no one could find anything fundamentally wrong with the Floyd-Jolson Maneuver. (That name was also unfair: he had insisted that Jolson get all the credit, but no one had listened. And Mihailovich had said: "Aren't you prepared to share the blame?")

The first test would be in twenty minutes, when Old Faithful rather belatedly greeted the dawn. But even if *that* worked, and the propellant tanks started to fill with sparkling pure water rather that the muddy slurry Captain Smith had predicted, the road to Europa was still not open.

A minor, but not unimportant, factor was the wishes of the distin-

guished passengers. They had expeected to be home within two weeks;
now, to their surprise and in some cases consternation, they were faced
with the prospect of a dangerous mission halfway across the Solar System
—and, even if it succeeded, no firm date for a return to Earth.

Willis was distraught; all his schedules would be totally wrecked. He
drifted around muttering about lawsuits, but no one expressed the slightest
sympathy.

Greenberg, on the other hand, was ecstatic; now he would really be in
the space business again! And Mihailovich—who spent a lot of time noisily
composing in his far from sound proof cabin, was almost equally delighted. He was sure that the diversion would inspire him to new heights of
creativity.

Maggie M was philosophical: "If it can save a lot of lives," she said,
looking pointedly at Willis, "how can anyone possibly object?"

As for Yva Merlin—Floyd made a special effort to explain matters to
her, and discovered that she understood the situation remarkably well.
And it was Yva, to his utter astonishment, who asked the question to
which no one else seemed to have paid much attention: "Suppose the
Europans don't want us to land—even to rescue our friends?"

Floyd looked at her in frank amazement; even now, he still found it
difficult to accept her as a real human being, and never knew when she
would come out with some brilliant insight or utter stupidity.

"That's a very good question, Yva. Believe me, I'm working on it."

He was telling the truth; he could never lie to Yva Merlin. That, somehow, would be an act of sacrilege.

The first wisps of vapor were appearing over the mouth of the geyser. They
shot upward and away in their unnatural vacuum trajectories, and evapo-
rated swiftly in the fierce sunlight.

Old Faithful coughed again and cleared its throat. A snowy-white—and
surprisingly compact—column of ice crystals and water droplets climbed
swiftly toward the sky. All one's terrestrial instincts expected it to topple
and fall, but of course it did not. It continued onward and upward, spreading only slightly, until it merged into the vast, glowing envelope of the
comet's still-expanding coma. Floyd noted, with satisfaction, that the pipeline was beginning to shake as fluid rushed into it.

Ten minutes later, there was a council of war on the bridge. Captain
Smith, still in a huff, acknowledged Floyd's presence with a slight nod; his
Number Two, a little embarrassed, did all the talking.

"Well, it works, surprisingly well. At this rate, we can fill our tanks in
twenty hours—though we may have to go out and anchor the pipe more
securely."

"What about the dirt?" someone asked.

The second officer held up a transparent squeezebulb holding a colorless liquid.

"The filters got rid of everything down to a few microns. To be on the safe side, we'll run through them twice, cycling from one tank to another. No swimming pool, I'm afraid, until we pass Mars."

That got a much-needed laugh, and even the captain relaxed a little.

"We'll run up the engines at minimum thrust to check that there are no operational anomalies with Halley H_2O. If there are, we'll forget the whole idea, and head home on good old Moon water, FOB Aristarchus."

There was one of those "party silences" where everyone waits simultaneously for someone else to speak. Then Captain Smith broke the embarrassing hiatus.

"As you all know," he said, "I'm very unhappy with the whole idea. In fact—"He changed course abruptly; it was equally well known that he had considered sending Sir Lawrence his resignation, though in the circumstances that would have been a somewhat pointless gesture.

"But a couple of things have happened in the last few hours. The owner agrees with the project—*if* no fundamental objections emerge from our tests. And—this is the big surprise, and I don't know any more about it than you do—the World Space Council has not only okayed but *requested* that we make the diversion, underwriting any expenses incurred. Your guess is as good as mine.

"But I still have one worry—" He looked doubtfully at the little bulb of water, which Heywood Floyd was now holding up to the light and shaking gently. "I'm an engineer, not a damn chemist. This stuff *looks* clean—but what will it do to the tank linings?"

Floyd never quite understood why he acted as he did; such rashness was completely uncharacteristic. Perhaps he was simply impatient with the whole debate and wanted to get on with the job. Or perhaps he felt that the captain needed a little stiffening of the moral fiber.

With one quick movement, he flicked open the stopcock and squirted approximately 20 ccs of Halley's comet down his throat.

"There's your answer, Captain," he said, when he had finished swallowing.

"And *that*," said the ship's doctor half an hour later, "was one of the silliest exhibitions I've ever seen. Don't you know that there are cyanides and cyanogens and God knows what else in that stuff?"

"Of course I do." Floyd laughed. "I've seen the analyses—just a few parts in a million. Nothing to worry about. But I did have one surprise," he added ruefully.

"And what was that?"

"If you could ship this stuff back to Earth, you could make a fortune selling it as Halley's Patent Purgative."

34 · Car Wash

Now that they were committed, the whole atmosphere aboard *Universe* had changed. There was no more argument; everyone was cooperating to the utmost, and very few people had much sleep for the next two rotations of the nucleus—a hundred hours of Earth time.

The first Halley day was devoted to a still rather cautious tapping of Old Faithful, but when the geyser subsided toward nightfall the technique had been thoroughly mastered. More than a thousand tons of water had been taken aboard; the next period of daylight would be ample for the rest.

Heywood Floyd kept out of the captain's way, not wishing to press his luck; in any event, Smith had a thousand details to attend to. But the calculation of the new orbit was not among them; that had been checked and rechecked on Earth.

There was no doubt, now, that the concept was brilliant, and the savings even greater than Jolson had claimed. By refueling on Halley, *Universe* had eliminated the two major orbit changes involved in the rendezvous with Earth; she could now go straight to her goal, under maximum acceleration, saving many weeks. Despite the possible risks, everyone now applauded the scheme.

Well, almost everyone.

On Earth, the swiftly organized "Hands off Halley!" society was indignant. Its members (a mere 236, but they knew how to drum up publicity) did not consider the rifling of a celestial body justified, even to save lives. They refused to be placated even when it was pointed out that *Universe* was merely borrowing material that the comet was about to lose anyway.

It was, they argued, the principle of the thing. Their angry communiques gave much-needed light relief aboard *Universe*.

Cautious as ever, Captain Smith ran the first low-powered tests with one of the attitude-control thrustors; if this became unserviceable, the ship could manage without it. There were no anomalies; the engine behaved exactly as if it were running on the best distilled water from the lunar mines.

Then he tested the central main engine, Number one; if *that* was damaged, there would be no loss of maneuverability—only of total thrust. The ship would still be fully controllable, but with the four remaining outboards alone, peak acceleration would be down by twenty percent.

Again, there were no problems; even the skeptics started being polite to Heywood Floyd, and Second Officer Jolson was no longer a social outcast.

The lift-off was scheduled late in the afternoon, just before Old Faithful was due to subside. (Would it still be there to greet the next visitors in seventy-six years time? Floyd wondered. Perhaps; there were hints of its existence even back on the 1910 photographs.)

There was no countdown, in the dramatic old-time Cape Canaveral style. When he was quite satisfied that everything was shipshape, Captain Smith applied a mere five tons of thrust on Number One, and *Universe* drifted slowly upward and away from the heart of the comet.

The acceleration was modest, but the pyrotechnics were awe-inspiring—and, to most of the watchers, wholly unexpected. Until now, the jets from the main engines had been virtually invisible, being formed entirely of highly ionized oxygen and hydrogen. Even when—hundreds of kilometers away—the gases had cooled off enough to combine chemically, there was still nothing to be seen, because the reaction gave no light in the visible spectrum.

But now, *Universe* was climbing away from Halley on a column of incandescence too brilliant for the eye to look upon; it seemed almost a solid pillar of flame. Where the flame hit the ground, rock exploded upward and outward; as it departed forever, *Universe* was carving its signature, like a piece of cosmic grafitti, across the nucleus of Halley's Comet.

Most of the passengers, accustomed to climbing spaceward with no visible means of support, reacted with considerable shock. Floyd waited for the inevitable explanation; one of his minor pleasures was catching Willis in some scientific error, but this very seldom happened. And even when it did, Willis always had some very plausible excuse.

"Carbon," he said. "Incandescent carbon—exactly as in a candle flame —but slightly hotter."

"Slightly," murmured Floyd.

"We're no longer burning, if you'll excuse the word—" Floyd shrugged his shoulders "—pure water. Although it's been carefully filtered, there's a lot of colloidal carbon in it. As well as compounds that could only be removed by distillation."

"It's very impressive, but I'm a little worried," said Greenberg. "All that radiation—won't it affect the engines and heat the ship badly?"

It was a very good question, and it had caused some anxiety. Floyd waited for Willis to handle it; but that shrewd operator bounced the ball right back to him.

"I'd prefer Dr. Floyd to deal with that—after all, it was his idea."

"Jolson's, please. Good point, though. But it's no real problem; when we're under full thrust, all those fireworks will be a thousand kilometers behind us. We won't have to worry about them."

The ship was now hovering some two kilometers above the nucleus; had it not been for the glare of the exhaust, the whole sunlit face of the tiny world would have been spread out beneath. At this altitude—or distance—the column of Old Faithful had broadened slightly. It looked, Floyd suddenly recalled, like one of the giant fountains ornamenting Lake Geneva. He had not seen them for fifty years, and wondered if they still played there.

Captain Smith was testing the controls, slowly rotating the ship, then pitching and yawing it along the Y and Z axes. Everything seemed to be functioning perfectly.

"Mission Time Zero is ten minutes from now," he announced. "Point one gee for fifty hours; then point two until Turnaround—one hundred fifty hours from now." He paused to let that sink in; no other ship had ever attempted to maintain so high a continuous acceleration for so long. If *Universe* was not able to brake properly, she would also enter the history books as the first manned interstellar voyager.

The ship was now turning toward the horizontal—if that word could be used in this almost gravityless environment—and was pointing directly to the white column of mist and ice crystals still steadily spurting from the comet. *Universe* started to move toward it—

"What's he *doing*?" said Mihailovich anxiously.

Obviously anticipating such questions, the captain spoke again. He seemed to have completely recovered his good humor, and there was a hint of amusement in his voice.

"Just one little chore before we leave. Don't worry—I know exactly what I'm doing. And Number Two agrees with me—don't you?"

"Yessir—though I thought you were joking at first."

"What *is* going on up on the bridge?" asked Willis, for once at a loss.

Now the ship was starting a slow roll, while still moving at no more than a good walking speed toward the geyser. From this distance—now less than a hundred meters—it reminded Floyd still more closely of those far-off Geneva fountains.

Surely he's not taking us into it—

—but he was. *Universe* vibrated gently as it nuzzled its way into the rising column of foam. It was still rolling very slowly, as if it were drilling its way into the giant geyser. The video monitors and observation windows showed only a milky blankness.

The whole operation could not have lasted more than ten seconds; then they were out on the other side. There was a brief burst of spontaneous clapping from the officers on the bridge; but the passengers—even including Floyd—still felt somewhat put-upon.

"Now we're ready to go," said the captain, in tones of great satisfaction. "We have a nice, clean ship again."

During the next half hour, more than ten thousand amateur observers on Earth and Moon reported that the comet had doubled its brightness. The Comet Watch Network broke down completely under the overload, and the professional astronomers were furious.

But the public loved it, and a few days later *Universe* put on an even better show, a few hours before dawn.

Gaining speed by more than ten thousand kilometers an hour, every hour, the ship was now far inside the orbit of Venus. It would get even closer to the Sun before it made its perihelion passage—far more swiftly than any natural celestial body—and headed out toward Lucifer.

As it passed between Earth and Sun, the thousand-kilometer tail of incandescent carbon was easily visible as a fourth-magnitude star, showing appreciable movement against the constellations of the morning sky in the course of a single hour. At the very beginning of its rescue mission, *Universe* would be seen by more human beings, at the same moment, than any artifact in the history of the world.

35 · Adrift

The unexpected news that their sister ship *Universe* was on the way—and might arrive far sooner than anyone had dared to dream—had an effect upon the morale of *Galaxy*'s crew that could only be called euphoric. The mere fact that they were drifting helplessly on a strange ocean, surrounded by unknown monsters, suddenly seemed of minor importance.

As did the monsters themselves, though they made interesting appearances from time to time. The giant "sharks" were sighted occasionally but never came near the ship, even when garbage was dumped overboard. This was quite surprising; it strongly suggested that the great beasts—unlike their terrestrial counterparts—had a good system of communication. Perhaps they were more closely allied to dolphins than to sharks.

There were many schools of smaller fish, which no one would have given a second glance in a market on Earth. After several attempts, one of the officers—a keen angler—managed to catch one with an unbaited hook. He never brought it in through the airlock—the captain would not have permitted it, anyway—but measured and photographed it carefully before returning it to the sea.

The proud sportsman had to pay a price for this trophy, however. The partial-pressure spacesuit he had worn during the exercise had the characteristic rotten-eggs stink of hydrogen sulfide when he brought it back into the ship, and he became the butt of innumerable jokes. It was yet another reminder of an alien, and implacably hostile, biochemistry.

Despite the pleas of the scientists, no further angling was allowed. They could watch and record, but not collect. And anyway, it was pointed out, they were planetary geologists, not naturalists. No one had thought of bringing formalin—which probably would not work here in any event.

Once the ship drifted for several hours through floating mats or sheets of some bright green material. It formed ovals, about ten meters across, and all of approximately the same size. *Galaxy* plowed through them without resistance, and they swiftly reformed behind her. It was guessed that they were colonial organisms of some kind.

And one morning, the officer of the watch was startled when a periscope rose out of the water and he found himself staring into a mild, blue eye that, he said when he had recovered, looked like a sick cow's. It regarded him sadly for a few moments, without much apparent interest, then slowly returned to the ocean.

Nothing seemed to move very fast here, and the reason was obvious. This was still a low-energy world—there was none of the free oxygen that allowed the animals of Earth to live by a series of continuous explosions, from the moment they started to breathe at birth. Only the "shark" of the first encounter had shown any sign of violent activity—in its last, dying spasm.

Perhaps that was good news for men. Even if they were encumbered with spacesuits, there was probably nothing on Europa that could catch them—even if it wanted to.

Captain Laplace found wry amusement in handing over the operation of his ship to the purser; he wondered if this situation was unique in the annals of space and sea.

Not that there was a great deal that Mr. Lee could do. *Galaxy* was floating vertically, one-third out of the water, heeling slightly before a wind that was driving it at a steady five knots. There were only a few leaks below the waterline, easily handled. Equally important, the hull was still airtight.

Although most of the navigation equipment was useless, they knew exactly where they were. Ganymede gave them an accurate fix on their emergency beacon every hour, and if *Galaxy* kept to her present course she would make landfall on a large island within the next three days. If she missed that, she would head on out to the open sea and eventually reach the tepidly boiling zone immediately underneath Lucifer. Though not necessarily catastrophic, that was a most unattractive prospect; Acting-Captain Lee spent much of his time thinking of ways to avoid it.

Sails—even if he had suitable material and rigging—would make very little difference to their course. He had lowered improvised sea anchors down to five hundred meters, looking for currents that might be useful, and finding none. Nor had he found the bottom; it lay unknown kilometers farther down.

Perhaps that was just as well; it protected them from the submarine quakes that continually wracked this new ocean. Sometimes *Galaxy* would shake as if struck by a giant hammer, as a shockwave went racing by. In a few hours, a *tsunami* dozens of metres high would crash upon some Europan shore; but here in deep water the deadly waves were little more than ripples.

Several times, sudden vortexes were observed at a distance; they looked quite dangerous—maelstroms that might even suck *Galaxy* down to unknown depths—but luckily they were too far off to do more than make the ship spin around a few times in the water.

And just once, a huge bubble of gas rose and burst only a hundred meters away. It was most impressive, and everyone seconded the doctor's heartfelt comment: "Thank God we can't smell it."

It is surprising how quickly the most bizarre situation can become routine. Within a few days, life aboard *Galaxy* had settled down to a steady routine, and Captain Laplace's main problem was keeping the crew occupied. There was nothing worse for morale than idleness, and he wondered how the skippers of the old windjammers had kept their men busy on those interminable voyages. They couldn't have spent *all* their time scrambling up the rigging or cleaning the decks.

He had the opposite problem with the scientists. They were always proposing tests and experiments, which had to be carefully considered before they could be approved. And if he allowed it, they would have monopolized the ship's now-very-limited communications channels.

The main antenna complex was now being battered around at the waterline, and *Galaxy* could no longer talk directly to Earth. Everything had to be relayed through Ganymede, on a bandwidth of a few miserable megahertz. A single live video channel preempted everything else, and he had to resist the clamor of the terrestrial networks. Not that they would have a great deal to show their audiences except open sea, cramped ship interiors, and a crew that, though in good spirits, was becoming steadily more hirsute.

An unusual amount of traffic seemed directed to Second Officer Floyd, whose encrypted responses were so brief that they could not have contained much information. Laplace finally decided to have a talk to the young man.

"Mr. Floyd," he said, in the privacy of his cabin. "I'd appreciate it if you would enlighten me about your part-time occupation."

Floyd looked embarrassed, and clutched at the table as the ship rocked slightly in a sudden gust.

"I wish I could, sir, but I'm not permitted."

"By whom, may I ask?"

"Frankly, I'm not sure."

That was perfectly true. He suspected it was ASTROPOL, but the two quietly impressive gentlemen who had briefed him on Ganymede had unaccountably failed to provide this information.

"As captain of this ship—*especially* in the present circumstances—I would like to know what's going on here. If we get out of this, I'm going to spend the next few years of my life at Courts of Inquiry. And you'll probably be doing the same."

Floyd managed a wry grin. "Hardly worth being rescued, is it, sir? All I know is that some high-level agency expected trouble on this mission, but didn't know what form it would take. I was just told to keep my eyes open. I'm afraid I didn't do much good, but I imagine I was the only qualified person they could get hold of in time."

"I don't think you can blame yourself. Who would have imagined that Rosie—"

The captain paused, struck by a sudden thought. "Do you suspect anyone else?" He felt like adding "Me, for instance?" but the situation was already sufficiently paranoic.

Floyd looked thoughtful, then apparently came to a decision. "Perhaps I should have spoken to you before, sir, but I know how busy you've been. I'm sure Dr. van der Berg is involved somehow. He's a Mede, of course; they're odd people, and I don't really understand them." Or like them, he might have added. Too clannish—not really friendly to offworlders. Still, one could hardly blame them; all pioneers trying to tame a new wilderness were probably much the same.

"van der Berg—hmm. What about the other scientists?"

"They've been checked, of course. All perfectly legitimate, and nothing unusual about any of them."

That was not altogether true. Dr. Simpson had more wives than was strictly legal, at least at one time, and Dr. Higgins had a large collection of most curious books. Second Officer Floyd was not quite sure why he had been told all this; perhaps his mentors merely wanted to impress him with their omniscience. He decided that working for ASTROPOL (or whoever it was) had some entertaining fringe benefits.

"Very well," said the captain, dismissing the amateur agent. "But please keep me informed if you discover anything—*anything at all*—that might affect the safety of the ship."

In the present circumstances, it was hard to imagine what that might be. Any further hazards seemed slightly superfluous.

36 · The Alien
Shore

Even twenty-four hours before they sighted the island, it was still not certain whether *Galaxy* would miss it and be blown on out into the emptiness of the central ocean. Her position, as observed by the Ganymede radar, was plotted on a large chart that everyone aboard examined anxiously several times a day.

Even if the ship did reach land, her problems might be just beginning. She might be pounded to pieces on a rocky coast rather than gently deposited on some conveniently shelving beach.

Acting-Captain Lee was keenly aware of all these possibilities. He had once been shipwrecked himself, in a cabin cruiser whose engines had failed at a critical moment off the island of Bali. There had been little danger, though a good deal of drama, and he had no wish to repeat the experience —especially as there was no coast guard here to come to the rescue.

There was a truly cosmic irony in their plight. Here they were, aboard one of the most advanced transportation devices ever made by man— capable of crossing the Solar System!—yet now they could not deflect it more than a few meters from its course. Nevertheless, they were not completely helpless; Lee still had a few cards to play.

On this sharply curving world, the island was only five kilometers away when they first sighted it. To Lee's great relief, there were none of the cliffs he had feared; nor, on the other hand, was there any sign of the beach he had hoped for. The geologists had warned him that he was a few million years too early to find sand here; the mills of Europa, grinding slowly, had not yet had time to do their work.

As soon as it was certain they would hit the land, Lee gave orders to pump out *Galaxy*'s main tanks, which he had deliberately flooded soon after touchdown. Then followed a very uncomfortable few hours, during which at least a quarter of the crew took no further interest in the proceedings.

Galaxy rose higher and higher in the water, oscillating more and more wildly—then tumbled with a mighty splash, to lie along the surface like the corpse of a whale, in the bad old days when the catcher-boats pumped them full of air to stop their sinking. When he saw how the ship was lying, Lee adjusted her buoyancy again, until she was slightly stern-down and the forward bridge was just clear of the water.

As he expected, *Galaxy* then swung broadside-on to the wind. Another quarter of the crew became incapacitated then, but Lee had enough helpers to get out the sea anchor he had prepared for this final act. It was merely an improvised raft, made of empty boxes lashed together, but its drag caused the ship to point toward the approaching land.

Now they could see that they were heading—with agonizing slowness— toward a narrow stretch of beach covered with small boulders. If they could not have sand, this was the best alternative . .

The bridge was already over the beach when *Galaxy* grounded, and Lee played his last card. He had made only a single test run, not daring to do more in case the abused machinery failed.

For the last time, *Galaxy* extended her landing gear. There was a grinding and shuddering as the pads on the underside dug their way into the alien surface. Now she was securely anchored against the winds and waves of this tideless ocean.

There was no doubt that *Galaxy* had found her final resting place—and, all too possibly, that of her crew.

V
Through
the
Asteroids

37 · Star

And now *Universe* was moving so swiftly that its orbit no longer even remotely resembled that of any natural object in the Solar System. Mercury, closest to the Sun, barely exceeds fifty kilometers a second at perihelion; *Universe* had reached twice that speed in the first day—and at only half the acceleration it would achieve when it was lighter by several thousand tons of water.

For a few hours, as they passed inside its orbit, Venus was the brightest of all heavenly bodies, next to the Sun and Lucifer. Its tiny disk was just visible to the naked eye, but even the ship's most powerful telescopes showed no markings whatever. Venus guarded her secrets as jealously as Europa.

By going still closer to the Sun—well inside the orbit of Mercury—*Universe* was not merely taking a shortcut, but was also getting a free boost from the Sun's gravitational field. Because Nature always balances her books, the Sun lost some velocity in the transaction; but the effect would not be measurable for a few thousand years.

Captain Smith used the ship's perihelion passage to restore some of the prestige his foot-dragging had cost him.

"Now you know," he said, "exactly *why* I flew the ship through Old Faithful. If we hadn't washed all that dirt off the hull, by this time we'd be badly overheating. In fact, I doubt if the thermal controls could have handled the load—it's already ten times Earth level." Looking—through filters that were almost black—at the hideously swollen Sun, his passengers could easily believe him. They were all more than happy when it had shrunk back to normal size—and continued to dwindle astern as *Universe* sliced across the orbit of Mars, outward bound on the final leg of its mission.

The Famous Five had all adjusted, in their various ways, to the unexpected change in their lives. Mihailovich was composing copiously and noisily, and was seldom seen except when he emerged at meals, to tell outrageous stories and tease all available victims, especially Willis. Greenberg had elected himself, no one dissenting, an honorary crew member, and spent much of his time on the bridge.

Maggie M viewed the situation with rueful amusement.

"Writers," she remarked, "are always saying what a lot of work they could do if they were only in some place with no interruptions—no engagements; lighthouses and prisons are their favorite examples. So I can't complain—except that my requests for research material keep getting delayed by high-priority messages."

Even Victor Willis had now come to much the same conclusion; he too was busily at work on sundry long-range projects. And he had an additional reason to keep to his cabin; it would still be several weeks before he looked as if he had forgotten to shave.

Yva Merlin spent hours every day in the entertainment center, catching up—as she readily explained—with her favorite classics. It was fortunate that *Universe*'s library and projection facilities had been installed in time for the voyage; though the collection was still relatively small, there was sufficient for several lifetimes of viewing.

All the famous works of visual art were there, right back to the flickering dawn of the cinema. Yva knew most of them and was happy to share her knowledge.

Floyd, of course, enjoyed listening to her, because then she became alive —an ordinary human being, not an icon. He found it both sad and fascinating that only through an artificial universe of video images could she establish contact with the real world.

One of the strangest experiences of Heywood Floyd's fairly eventful life was sitting in semidarkness just behind Yva, somewhere outside the orbit of Mars, while they watched the original *Gone With the Wind* together. There were moments when he could see her famous profile silhouetted against that of Vivien Leigh, and could compare the two—though it was impossible to say that one actress was better than the other; both were *sui generis*.

When the lights went up, he was astonished to see that Yva was crying. He took her hand and said tenderly: "I cried too, when Bonny died."

Yva managed a faint smile.

"I was really crying for Vivien," she said. "While we were shooting Two, I read a lot about her—she had such a tragic life. And talking about her, right out here between the planets, reminds me of something that

Larry said when he brought the poor thing back from Ceylon after her nervous breakdown. He told his friends: 'I've married a woman from outer space.' "

Yva paused for a moment, and another tear trickled (rather theatrically, Floyd could not help thinking) down her cheek.

"And here's something even stranger. She made her last movie exactly a hundred years ago—and do you know what it was?"

"Go on—surprise me again."

"I expect it will surprise Maggie—if she's really writing the book she keeps threatening us with. Vivien's very last film was *Ship of Fools*."

38 · Icebergs
of Space

Now that they had so much unexpected time on their hands, Captain
Smith had finally agreed to give Victor Willis the long-delayed interview
that was part of his contract. Victor himself had kept putting it off, owing
to what Mihailovich persisted in calling his amputation. As it would be
many months before he could regenerate his public image, he had finally
decided to do the interview off-camera; the studio on Earth could fake him
in later with library shots.

They had been sitting in the captain's still only partly furnished cabin,
enjoying one of the excellent wines that apparently made up much of
Victor's baggage allowance. As *Universe* would cut its drive and start
coasting within the next few hours, this would be the last opportunity for
several days. Weightless wine, Victor maintained, was an abomination; he
refused to put any of his precious vintages into plastic squeeze-bulbs.

"This is Victor Willis, aboard the spaceship *Universe* at 1830 on Friday,
15 July 2061. Though we're not yet at the midpoint of our journey, we're
already far beyond the orbit of Mars, and have almost reached our maximum velocity. Which is, Captain?"

"One thousand fifty kilometers a second."

"More than a thousand kilometers a second—almost four *million* kilometers an hour!"

Victor Willis' surprise sounded perfectly genuine; no one would have
guessed that he knew the orbital parameters almost as well as did the
captain. But one of his strengths was his ability to put himself in the place
of his viewers, and not only to anticipate their questions but to arouse their
interest.

"That's right," the captain answered with quiet pride. "We are traveling twice as fast as any human beings since the beginning of time."

That should have been one of my lines, thought Victor; he did not like his subject to get ahead of him. But, good professional that he was, he quickly adapted.

He paused as if to consult his famous little memopad, with its sharply directional screen whose display only he could see.

"Every twelve seconds, we're traveling the diameter of Earth. Yet it will still take us another ten days to reach Jupe—ah, Lucifer! That gives some idea of the scale of the Solar System—

"Now, Captain, this is a delicate subject, but I've had a lot of questions about it during the last week."

Oh no, groaned Smith. Not the zero-gravity toilets again!

"At this very moment, we are passing right through the heart of the asteroid belt—"

(I wish it *was* the toilets, thought Smith.)

"—and though no spaceship has ever been seriously damaged by a collision, aren't we taking quite a risk? After all, there are literally millions of bodies, down to the size of beachballs, orbiting in this section of space. And only a few thousand have been charted."

"More than a few: over ten thousand."

"But there are millions we don't know about."

"That's true; but it wouldn't help us much if we *did*."

"What do you mean?"

"There's nothing we can do about them."

"Why not?"

Captain Smith paused for careful thought. Willis was right—this was indeed a delicate subject; Head Office would rap his knuckles smartly if he said anything to discourage potential customers.

"First of all, space is so enormous that even here—as you said, right in the heart of the asteroid belt—the chance of collision is infinitesimal. We've been hoping to show you an asteroid—the best we can do is Hanuman, a miserable three hundred meters across—but the nearest we get to it is a quarter million kilometers."

"But Hanuman is gigantic, compared to all the unknown debris that's floating round out here. Aren't you worried about that?"

"About as worried as you are at being struck by lightning on Earth."

"As a matter of fact, I once had a narrow escape, on Pike's Peak in Colorado—the flash and the bang were simultaneous. But you admit that the danger does exist—and aren't we increasing the risk by the enormous speed we're traveling?"

Willis, of course, knew the answer perfectly well; once again he was putting himself in the place of his legions of unknown listeners on the planet that was getting a thousand kilometers farther away with every passing second.

"It's hard to explain without mathematics," said the captain (how many times he had used that phrase, even when it wasn't true!), "but there's no simple relationship between speed and risk. To hit *anything* at spacecraft velocities would be catastrophic; if you're standing next to an atomic bomb when it goes off, it makes no difference whether it's in the kiloton or megaton class."

That was not exactly a reasurring statement, but it was the best he could do. Before Willis could press the point further, he continued hastily:

"And let me remind you that any—er—slight extra risk we may be running is in the best of causes. A single hour may save lives."

"Yes, I'm sure we all appreciate that." Willis paused; he thought of adding "And of course I'm in the same boat," but decided against it. It might sound immodest—not that modesty had ever been his strong suit. And anyway, he could hardly make a virtue of a necessity; he had very little alternative now, unless he decided to walk home.

"All this," he continued, "brings me to another point. Do you know what happened just a century and a half ago on the North Atlantic?"

"In 1911?"

"Well, actually 1912—"

Captain Smith guessed what was coming, refused to cooperate, with a pretense of ignorance.

"I suppose you mean the *Titanic*," he said.

"Precisely," answered Willis, gamely concealing his disappointment. "I've had at least twenty reminders from people who think *they're* the only one who's spotted the parallel."

"What parallel? The *Titanic* was running unacceptable risks, merely trying to break a record."

He almost added "And she didn't have enough lifeboats," but luckily checked himself in time, when he recalled that the ship's one-and-only shuttle could carry not more than five passengers. If Willis took him up on *that*, it would involve altogether too many explanations.

"Well, I grant that the analogy is far fetched. But there's another striking parallel that *everyone* points out. Do you happen to know the name of *Titanic*'s first and last captain?"

"I haven't the faintest—" began Captain Smith. Then his jaw dropped.

"Precisely," said Victor Willis, with a smile that it would be charitable to call smug.

Captain Smith would willingly have strangled all those amateur researchers. But he could hardly blame his parents for bequeathing him the commonest of English names.

39 · The Captain's Table

It was a pity that viewers on (and off) Earth could not have enjoyed the less formal discussions aboard *Universe*. Shipboard life had now settled down to a steady routine, punctuated by a few regular landmarks—of which the most important, and certainly the most long-established, was the Captain's Table.

At 1800 hours exactly, the six passengers and five of the officers not on duty would join Captain Smith for dinner. There was, of course, none of the formal dress that had been mandatory aboard the floating palaces of the North Atlantic, but there was usually some attempt at sartorial novelty. Yva could always be relied upon to produce some new broach, ring, necklace, hair ribbon, or perfume from an apparently inexhaustible supply.

If the drive was on, the meal would begin with soup; but if the ship was coasting and weightless, there would be a selection of hors d'oeuvres. In either event, before the main course was served Captain Smith would report the latest news—or try to dispel the latest rumors, usually fueled by newscasts from Earth or Ganymede.

Accusations and countercharges were flying in all directions, and the most fantastic theories had been proposed to account for *Galaxy*'s hijacking. A finger had been pointed at every secret organization known to exist and many that were purely imaginary. All the theories, however, had one thing in common. Not one of them could suggest a plausible motive.

The mystery had been compounded by the one fact that had emerged. Strenuous detective work by ASTROPOL had established the surprising fact that the late "Rose McMahon" was really Ruth Mason, born in North London, recruited to the Metropolitan Police—and then, after a promising start, dismissed for racist activities. She had emigrated to Africa—and vanished. Obviously she had become involved in that unlucky continent's political underground. Shaka was frequently mentioned, and as frequently denied by the USSA.

What all this could possibly have to do with Europa was endlessly, and fruitlessly, debated around the table—especially when Maggie M confessed that at one time she had been planning a novel about Shaka, from the viewpoint of one of the Zulu despot's thousand unfortunate wives. But the more she researched the project, the more repellent it became. "By the time I abandoned Shaka," she wryly admitted, "I knew exactly what a modern German feels about Hitler."

Such personal revelations became more and more common as the voyage proceeded. When the main meal was over, one of the group would be given the floor for thirty minutes. Between them, they had a dozen lifetimes of experience, on as many heavenly bodies, so it would be hard to find a better source of after-dinner tales.

The least effective speaker was, somewhat surprisingly, Victor Willis. He was frank enough to admit it, and to give the reason.

"I'm so used," he said, almost but not quite apologetically, "to performing for an audience of millions that I find it hard to interact with a friendly little group like this."

"Could you do better if it wasn't friendly?" asked Mihailovich, always anxious to be helpful. "That could be easily arranged."

Yva, on the other hand, turned out to be better than expected, even though her memories were confined entirely to the world of entertainment. She was particularly good on the famous—and infamous—directors she had worked with, especially David Griffin.

"Was it true," asked Maggie M, doubtless thinking of Shaka, "that he hated women?"

"Not at all," Yva answered promptly. "He just hated *actors*. He didn't believe they were human beings."

Mihailovich's reminiscences also covered a somewhat limited territory —the great orchestras and ballet companies, famous conductors and composers, and their innumerable hangers-on. But he was so full of hilarious stories of backstage intrigues and liaisons, and accounts of sabotaged first nights and mortal feuds among *prima donnas*, that he kept even his most unmusical listeners convulsed with laughter and was willingly granted extra time.

Colonel Greenberg's matter-of-fact accounts of extraordinary events could hardly have provided a greater contrast. The first landing at Mercury's—relatively—temperate South Pole had been so thoroughly reported that there was little new to be said about it; the question that interested everyone was: "When will we return?" That was usually followed by: "Would you like to go back?"

"If they ask me to, of course I'll go," Greenberg answered. "But I rather think that Mercury is going to be like the Moon. Remember—we landed there in 1969—and didn't go back again for half a lifetime. Anyway, Mercury isn't as useful as the Moon—though perhaps one day it may be. There's no water there; of course, it was quite a surprise to find any on the Moon. Or I should say *in* the Moon . . .

"Though it wasn't as glamorous as landing on Mercury, I did a more important job setting up the Aristarchus mule train."

"Mule train?"

"Yep. Before the big equatorial launcher was built and they started shooting the ice straight into orbit, we had to haul it from the pit-head to the Imbrium Spaceport. That meant leveling a road across the lava plains and bridging quite a few crevasses. The Ice Road, we called it—only three hundred kilometers, but it took several lives to build . . .

"The 'mules' were eight-wheeled tractors with huge tires and independent suspension: they towed up to a dozen trailers, with a hundred tons of ice apiece. Used to travel by night—no need to shield the cargo then.

"I rode with them several times. The trip took about six hours—we weren't out to break speed records—then the ice would be offloaded into big, pressurized tanks, waiting for sunrise. As soon as it melted, it would be pumped into the ships.

"The Ice Road is still there, of course, but only the tourists use it now. If they're sensible, they'll drive by night, as we used to do. It was pure magic, with the full Earth almost directly overhead, so brilliant that we seldom used our own lights. And although we could talk to our friends whenever we wanted to, we often switched off the radio and left it to the automatics to tell them we were okay. We just wanted to be alone, in that great shining emptiness—while it was still there, because we knew it wouldn't last.

"Now they're building the Teravolt quark-smasher, running right around the Equator, and domes are going up all over Imbrium and Serenitatis. But we knew the *real* lunar wilderness, exactly as Armstrong and Aldrin saw it—before you could buy 'Wish you were here' cards in the post office at Tranquillity Base."

40 · Monsters
From Earth

"... lucky you missed the annual ball: believe it or not, it was just as grisly as last year's. And once again our resident mastodon, dear Miz Wilkinson, managed to crush her partner's toes, even on the half-gee dance floor.

"Now some business. Since you won't be back for months, instead of a couple of weeks, Admin is looking lustfully at your apartment—good neighborhood, near downtown shopping area, splendid view of Earth on clear days, etc., etc.—and suggests a sublet until you return. Seems a good deal, and will save you a lot of money. We'll collect any personal effects you'd like stored . . .

"Now this Shaka business. We know you love pulling our legs, but frankly Jerry and I were horrified! I can see why Maggie M turned him down—yes, of course we've read her *Olympic Lusts*—very enjoyable, but too feminist for us . . .

"What a monster—I can understand why they've called a gang of African terrorists after him. Fancy executing his warriors if they got married! And killing all the poor cows in his wretched empire, just because they were female! Worst of all—those horrid spears he invented; shocking manners, jabbing them into people you've not been properly introduced to . . .

"And what a ghastly advertisement for us feys! Almost enough to make one want to switch. We've always claimed that we're gentle and kind-hearted (as well as madly talented and artistic, of course) but now you've made us look into some of the so-called Great Warriors (as if there was anything great about killing people!) we're almost ashamed of the company we've been keeping . . .

"Yes, we *did* know about Hadrian and Alexander—but we certainly *didn't* know about Richard the Lion Heart and Saladin. Or Julius Caesar —though he was *everything*—ask Anthony as well as Cleo. Or Frederick the Great, who does have some redeeming features; look how he treated old Bach.

"When I told Jerry that at least Napoleon is an exception—we don't have to be saddled with *him*—do you know what he said? 'I bet Josephine was really a boy.' Try *that* on Yva.

"You've ruined our morale, you rascal, tarring us with that bloodstained brush (sorry about the mixed metaphor). You should have left us in happy ignorance . . .

"Despite that, we send our love, and so does Sebastian. Say hello to any Europans you meet. Judging by the reports from *Galaxy*, some of them would make very good partners for Miz Wilkinson."

41 · Memoirs of a Centenarian

Dr. Heywood Floyd preferred not to talk about the first mission to Jupiter and the second to Lucifer ten years later. It was all so long ago—and there was nothing he had not said a hundred times to congressional committees, Space Council boards, and media persons like Victor Willis.

Nevertheless, he had a duty to his fellow-passengers that could not be avoided. As the only living man to have witnessed the birth of a new sun—and a new solar system—they expected him to have some special understanding of the worlds they were now so swiftly approaching. It was a naive assumption; he could tell them far less about the Galilean satellites than the scientists and engineers who had been working there for more than a generation. When he was asked "What's it *really* like on Europa (or Ganymede, or Io, or Callisto . . .)?" he was liable to refer the inquirer, rather brusquely, to the voluminous reports available in the ship's library.

Yet there was one area where his experience was unique. Half a century later, he sometimes wondered if it had really happened, or whether he had been asleep aboard *Discovery* when David Bowman had appeared to him. Almost easier to believe that a spaceship could be haunted . . .

But he could not have been dreaming when the floating dust motes assembled themselves into that ghostly image of a man who should have been dead for a dozen years. Without the warning it had given him (how clearly he remembered that its lips were motionless, and the voice had come from the console speaker), *Leonov* and all aboard would have been vaporized in the detonation of Jupiter.

"Why did he do it?" Floyd answered during one of the afterdinner sessions. "I've puzzled over that for fifty years. Whatever he became, after he went out in *Discovery*'s space pod to investigate the monolith, he must still have had some links with the human race; he was not completely alien. We know that he returned to Earth—briefly—because of that orbiting bomb incident. And there's strong evidence that he visited both his mother and his old girlfriend; that's not the action of—of an entity that had discarded all emotions."

"What do you suppose he is *now*?" asked Willis. "For that matter—*where* is he?"

"Perhaps that last question has no meaning—even for human beings. Do you know where *your* consciousness resides?"

"I've no use for metaphysics. Somewhere in the general area of my brain, anyway."

"When I was a young man," sighed Mihailovich, who had a talent for deflating the most serious discussions, "mine was about a meter lower down."

"Let's assume he's on Europa; we know there's a monolith there, and Bowman was certainly associated with it in some way—see how he relayed that warning."

"Do you think he also relayed the second one, telling us to stay away?"

"Which we are now going to ignore—"

"—in a good cause—"

Captain Smith, who was usually content to let the discussion go where it wished, made one of his rare interjections.

"Dr. Floyd," he said thoughtfully, "you're in a unique position, and we should take advantage of it. Bowman went out of his way to help you once. If he's still around, he may be willing to do so again. I worry a good deal about that 'Attempt no landings here' order. If he could assure us that it was—temporarily suspended, let's say—I'd be much happier."

There were several "hear, hears" around the table before Floyd answered.

"Yes, I've been thinking along the same lines. I've already told *Galaxy* to watch out for any—let's say, manifestations—in case he tries to make contact."

"Of course," said Yva, "he may be dead by now—if ghosts can die."

Not even Mihailovich had a suitable comment to this, but Yva obviously sensed that no one thought much of her contribution.

Undeterred, she tried again.

"Woody, dear," she said. "Why don't you simply give him a call on the radio? That's what it's for, isn't it?"

The idea had occurred to Floyd, but it had somehow seemed too naive to take seriously.

"I will," he said. "I don't suppose it will do any harm."

42 · Minilith

This time, Floyd was quite sure he was dreaming . . .

He had never been able to sleep well in zero gravity, and *Universe* was now coasting, unpowered, at maximum velocity. In two days it would start almost a week of steady deceleration, throwing away its enormous excess speed until it was able to rendezvous with Europa.

However many times he adjusted the restraining straps, they always seemed either too tight or too loose. He would have difficulty in breathing —or else he would find himself drifting out of his bunk.

Once he had awoken in midair and had flailed away for several minutes until, exhausted, he had managed to swim the few meters to the nearest wall. Not until then had he remembered that he should merely have waited; the room ventilating system would have soon pulled him to the exhaust grill without any exertion on his part. As a seasoned space traveler, he knew this perfectly well; his only excuse was simple panic.

But tonight he had managed to get everything right; probably when weight returned, he would have difficulty in readjusting to *that*. He had lain awake for only a few minutes, recapitulating the latest discussion at dinner, and had then fallen asleep.

In his dreams, he had continued the conversation around the table. There had been a few trifling changes, which he accepted without surprise. Willis, for example, had grown his beard back—though on only *one* side of his face. This, Floyd presumed, was in aid of some research project, though he found it difficult to imagine its purpose.

In any event, he had his own worries. He was defending himself against the criticisms of Space Administrator Millson, who had somewhat surprisingly joined their little group. Floyd wondered how he had come aboard *Universe* (could he possibly have stowed away?). The fact that Millson had been dead for at least forty years seemed much less important.

"Heywood," his old enemy was saying, "the White House is most upset."

"I can't imagine why."

"That radio message you've just sent to Europa. Did it have State Department clearance?"

"I didn't think it was necessary. I merely asked permission to land."

"Ah—but that's it. *Who* did you ask? Do we recognize the government concerned? I'm afraid it's all very irregular."

Millson faded away, still tut-tutting. *I'm very glad this is only a dream,* thought Floyd. *Now what?*

Well, I might have expected it. Hello, old friend. You come in all sizes, don't you? Of course, even TMA-1 couldn't have squeezed into my cabin —and its Big Brother could easily have swallowed Universe *in one gulp.*

The black monolith was standing—or floating—only two meters from his bunk. With an uncomfortable shock of recognition, Floyd realized that it was not only the same shape but also the same size as an ordinary tombstone. Although the resemblance had often been pointed out to him, until now the incongruity of scale had lessened the psychological impact. Now, for the first time, he felt the likeness was disquieting—even sinister. *I* know *this is only a dream—but at my age, I don't want any reminders . . .*

Anyway—what are you doing here? Do you bring a message from Dave Bowman? Are you Dave Bowman?

Well, I didn't really expect an answer; you weren't very talkative in the past, were you? But things always happened when you were around. Back in Tycho, sixty years ago, you sent that signal to Jupiter, to tell your makers that we'd dug you up. And look what you did to Jupiter when we got there a dozen years later!

What are you up to now?

VI
Haven

Demo

43 · Salvage

The first task confronting Captain Laplace and his crew, once they had grown accustomed to being on *terra firma*, was to reorient themselves. Everything on *Galaxy* was the wrong way round.

Spaceships are designed for two modes of operation—either no gravity at all, or, when the engines are thrusting, an up-and-down direction along the axis. But now *Galaxy* was lying almost horizontally, and all the floors had become walls. It was exactly as if they were trying to live in a lighthouse that had toppled onto its side; every single piece of furniture had to be moved, and at least fifty percent of the equipment was not functioning properly.

Yet in some ways this was a blessing in disguise, and Captain Laplace made the most of it. The crew was so busy rearranging *Galaxy*'s interior—giving priority to the plumbing—that he had few worries about morale. As long as the hull remained airtight and the muon generators continued to supply power, they were in no immediate danger; they merely had to survive for twenty days, and salvation would come from the skies in the shape of *Universe*. No one ever mentioned the possibility that the unknown powers that ruled Europa might object to a second landing. They had—as far as anyone knew—ignored the first; surely they would not interfere with a mission of mercy . . .

Europa itself, however, was now less cooperative. While *Galaxy* had been adrift on the open sea, it had been virtually unaffected by the quakes that continually wracked the little world. But now that the ship had become an all-too-permanent land structure, it was shaken every few hours by seismic disturbances. Had it touched down in the normal vertical position, by now it would certainly have been overturned.

The quakes were unpleasant rather than dangerous, but they gave nightmares to anyone who had experienced Tokyo '33 or Los Angeles '45. It did not help much to know that they followed a completely predictable pattern, rising to a peak of violence and frequency every three and a half days when Io came swinging past on its inner orbit. Nor was it much consolation to know that Europa's own gravitational tides were inflicting at least equal damage on Io.

After six days of grueling work, Captain Laplace was satisfied that *Galaxy* was as near shipshape as was possible in the circumstances. He declared a holiday—which most of the crew spent sleeping—and then drew up a schedule for their second week on the satellite.

The scientists, of course, wanted to explore the new world they had so unexpectedly entered. According to the radar maps that Ganymede had transmitted to them, the island was fifteen kilometers long and five wide; its maximum elevation was only a hundred meters—not high enough, someone had gloomily predicted, to avoid a really bad *tsunami*.

It was hard to imagine a more dismal and forbidding place; half a century of exposure to Europa's feeble winds and rains had done nothing to break up the pillow lava that covered half its surface or to soften the outcropping of granite that protruded through the rivers of frozen rock. But it was their home now, and they had to find a name for it.

Gloomy, downbeat suggestions like Hades, Inferno, Hell, Purgatory . . . were firmly vetoed by the captain; he wanted something cheerful. One surprising and quixotic tribute to a brave enemy was seriously considered before being rejected thirty-two to ten, with five abstentions: the island would *not* be called "Roseland" . . .

In the end, "Haven" won, unanimously.

44 · Endurance

"History never repeats itself—but historical situations recur."

As he made his daily report to Ganymede, Captain Laplace kept thinking of that phrase. It had been quoted by Margaret M'Bala—now approaching at almost a thousand kilometers every second—in a message of encouragement from *Universe* that he had been very happy to relay to his fellow castaways.

"Please tell Miss M'Bala that her little history lesson was extremely good for morale; she couldn't have thought of anything better to send us . . .

"Despite the inconvenience of having our walls and floors switched around, we're living in luxury compared to those old polar explorers. Some of us had heard of Ernest Shackleton, but we had no idea of the *Endurance* saga. To have been trapped on ice floes for over a year—then to spend the Antarctic winter in a cave—then to cross a thousand kilometers of sea in an open boat and to climb a range of unmapped mountains to reach the nearest human settlement!

"And yet that was only the beginning. What we find incredible—and inspiring—is that Shackleton went back four times to rescue his men on that little island—*and saved every one of them!* You can guess what that story's done to our spirits. I hope you can fax his book to us in your next transmission—we're all anxious to read it.

"And what would he have thought of *that!* Yes, we're infinitely better off than any of those old-time explorers. It's almost impossible to believe that, until well into the last century, they were completely cut off from the rest of the human race once they'd gone over the horizon. We should be ashamed at grumbling because light isn't fast enough and we can't talk to our friends in real-time—or that it takes a couple of hours to get replies from Earth . . . *They* had no contact for months—almost years! Again, Miss M'Bala—our sincerest thanks.

"Of course, all Earth explorers did have one considerable advantage over us; at least they could breathe the air. Our science team has been clamoring to go outside, and we've modified four spacesuits for EVAs of up to six hours. At this atmospheric pressure they won't need full suits—a waist seal is good enough—and I'm allowing two men to go out at a time, as long as they stay within sight of the ship.

"Finally, here's today's weather report. Pressure 250 bars, temperature steady at twenty-five degrees, wind gusting at up to thirty klicks from the west, usual one hundred percent overcast, quakes between one and three on open-ended Richter . . .

"You know, I never did like the sound of that 'open-ended'—especially now that Io's coming into conjunction again . . ."

45 · Mission

When people asked to see him together, it usually meant trouble, or at least some difficult decision. Captain Laplace had noticed that Floyd and van der Berg were spending a lot of time in earnest discussions, often with Second Officer Chang, and it was easy to guess what they were talking about. Yet their proposal still took him by surprise.

"You want to *go* to Mount Zeus! How—in an open boat? Has that Shackleton book gone to your head?"

Floyd looked slightly embarrassed; the captain was right on target. *South* had been an inspiration, in more ways than one.

"Even if we could build a boat, sir, it would take much too long . . . especially now that *Universe* looks like reaching us within ten days."

"And I'm not sure," added van der Berg, "that I'd care to sail on *this* Sea of Galilee; not all its inhabitants may have got the message that we're inedible."

"So that leaves only one alternative, doesn't it? I'm skeptical, but I'm willing to be convinced. Go on."

"We've discussed it with Mr. Chang, and he confirms that it can be done. Mount Zeus is only three hundred kilometers away; the shuttle can fly there in less than an hour."

"And find a place to land? As you doubtless recall, Mr. Chang wasn't very successful with *Universe*."

"No problem, sir. The *William Tsung*'s only a hundredth of our mass; even that ice could probably have supported it. We've been over the video records and found a dozen good landing sites."

"Besides," said van der Berg, "the pilot won't have a pistol pointed at him. That could help."

"I'm sure it will. But the big problem is at *this* end. How are you going to get the shuttle out of its garage? Can you rig a crane? Even in this gravity, it would be quite a load."

"No need to, sir. Mr. Chang can fly it out."

There was a prolonged silence while Captain Laplace contemplated, obviously without much enthusiasm, the idea of rocket motors firing *inside* his ship. The small hundred-ton shuttle *William Tsung*, more familiarly known as *Bill Tee*, was designed purely for orbital operations; normally, it would be pushed gently out of its "garage," and the engines would not operate until it was well away from the mother ship.

"Obviously you've worked all this out," said the captain grudgingly, "but what about the angle of take-off? Don't tell me you want to roll *Universe* over so that *Bill Tee* can pop straight up? The garage is halfway down one side; lucky it wasn't underneath when we grounded."

"The take-off will have to be at sixty degrees to the horizontal; the lateral thrusters can handle it."

"If Mr. Chang says so, I'll certainly believe him. But what will the firing do to the ship?"

"Well, it will wreck the garage interior—but it will never be used again, anyway. And the bulkheads are designed for accidental explosions, so there's no danger of damage to the rest of the ship. We'll have fire-fighting crews standing by, just in case."

It was a brilliant concept—no doubt of that. If it worked, the mission would not be a total failure. During the last week, Captain Laplace had given scarcely a moment's thought to the mystery of Mount Zeus, which had brought them to this predicament; only survival had mattered. But now there was hope, and leisure to think ahead. It would be worth taking some risks to find why this little world was the focus of so much intrigue.

46 · Shuttle

"Speaking from memory," said Dr. Anderson, "Goddard's first rocket flew about fifty meters. I wonder if Mr. Chang will beat that record."

"He'd better—or we'll *all* be in trouble."

Most of the science team had gathered in the observation lounge, and everyone was staring anxiously back along the hull of the ship. Although the entrance of the garage was not visible from this angle, they would see the *Bill Tee* soon enough, when—and if—it emerged.

There was no countdown; Chang was taking his time, making every possible check—and would fire when he felt like it. The shuttle had been stripped down to its minimum mass and was carrying just enough propellant for one hundred seconds of flight. If everything worked, that would be ample; if it didn't, more would not only be superfluous, but dangerous.

"Here we go," said Chang casually.

It was almost like a conjuring trick; everything happened so quickly that the eye was deceived. No one saw *Bill Tee* pop out of the garage, because it was hidden in a cloud of steam. When the cloud had cleared, the shuttle was already landing, two hundred meters away.

A great cheer of relief echoed through the lounge.

"He did it!" cried ex-Acting-Captain Lee. "He's broken Goddard's record—easily!"

Standing on its four stubby legs in the bleak Europan landscape, *Bill Tee* looked like a larger and even less elegant version of an Apollo lunar module. That was not, however, the thought that occurred to Captain Laplace as he looked out from the bridge.

It seemed to him that his ship was rather like a stranded whale that had managed a difficult birth in an alien element. He hoped that the new calf would survive.

Forty-eight very busy hours later, the *William Tsung* was loaded, checked out on a ten-kilometer circuit over the island—and ready to go. There was still plenty of time for the mission; by the most optimistic reckoning, *Universe* could not arrive for another three days, and the trip to Mount Zeus, even allowing for the deployment of Dr. van der Berg's extensive array of instruments, would take only six hours.

As soon as Second Officer Chang had landed, Captain Laplace called him to his cabin. The skipper looked, thought Chang, somewhat ill at ease.

"Good work, Walter—but of course that's only what we expect."

"Thanks, sir. So what's the problem?"

The captain smiled. A well-integrated crew could keep no secrets.

"Head Office, as usual. I hate to disappoint you, but I've had orders that only Dr. van der Berg and Second Officer Floyd are to make the trip."

"I get the picture," Chang answered, with a trace of bitterness. "What have you told them?"

"Nothing, yet; that's why I wanted to talk to you. I'm quite prepared to say that you're the only pilot who can fly the mission."

"They'll know that's nonsense; Floyd could do the job as well as I can. There's not the slightest risk—except for a malfunction, which could happen to anyone."

"I'd still be willing to stick my neck out, if you insist. After all, no one can stop me—and we'll all be heroes when we get back to Earth."

Chang was obviously doing some intricate calculations. He seemed rather pleased with the result.

"Replacing a couple of hundred kilos of payload with propellant gives us an interesting new option; I'd intended to mention it earlier, but there was no way *Bill Tee* could manage with all that extra gear *and* a full crew . . ."

"Don't tell me. The Great Wall."

"Of course; we could do a complete survey in one or two passes and find what it *really* is."

"I thought we had a very good idea, and I'm not sure if we should go near it. That might be pressing our luck."

"Perhaps. But there's another reason; to some of us, it's an even better one . . ."

"Go on."

"*Tsien*. It's only ten kilometers from the Wall. We'd like to drop a wreath there."

So *that* was what his officers had been discussing so solemnly; not for the first time, Captain Laplace wished he knew a little more Mandarin.

"I understand," he said quietly. "I'll have to think it over—and talk to van der Berg and Floyd, to see if they agree."

"And Head Office?"

"No, dammit. This will be *my* decision."

47 · Shards

"You'd better hurry," Ganymede Central had advised. "The next conjunction will be a bad one—*we'll* be triggering quakes as well as Io. And we don't want to scare you—but unless our radar's gone crazy, your mountain's sunk another hundred meters since the last check."

At that rate, thought van der Berg, Europa will be flat again in ten years. How much faster things happened here than on Earth; which was one reason why the place was so popular with geologists.

Now that he was strapped into the number-two position immediately behind Floyd and virtually surrounded by consoles of his own equipment, he felt a curious mixture of excitement and regret. In a few hours, the great intellectual adventure of his life would be over—one way or the other. Nothing that would ever happen again could possibly match it.

He did not have the slightest trace of fear; his confidence in both man and machine was complete. One unexpected emotion was a wry sense of gratitude to the late Rose McMahon; without her, he would never have had this opportunity, but might have gone, still uncertain, to his grave.

The heavily laden *Bill Tee* could barely manage one-tenth of a gravity at lift-off; it was not intended for this sort of work, but would manage much better on the homeward journey when it had deposited its cargo. It seemed to take ages to climb clear of *Galaxy*, and they had ample time to note the damage to the hull as well as signs of corrosion from the occasional mildly acid rains. While Floyd concentrated on the lift-off, van de Berg gave a quick report on the ship's condition from the viewpoint of a privileged observer. It seemed the right thing to do—even though, with any luck, *Galaxy*'s spaceworthiness would soon be of no further concern to anyone.

Now they could see the whole of Haven spread out beneath them, and van der Berg realized what a brilliant job Acting-Captain Lee had done when he beached the ship. There were only a few places where it could have been safely grounded; although a good deal of luck had also been involved, Lee had used wind and sea anchor to the best possible advantage.

The mists closed around them; *Bill Tee* was rising on a semiballistic trajectory to minimize drag, and there would be nothing to see except clouds for twenty minutes. A pity, thought van der Berg; I'm sure there must be some interesting creatures swimming around down there, and no one else may ever have a chance of seeing them . . .

"Coming up to engine cut-off," said Floyd. "Everything nominal."

"Very good, *Bill Tee*. No report of traffic at your altitude. You're still number one on the runway to land."

"Who's that joker?" asked van der Berg.

"Ronnie Lim. Believe it or not, that 'number one on the runway' goes back to Apollo."

van der Berg could understand why. There was nothing like the occasional touch of humor—providing it was not overdone—to relieve the strain when men were involved in some complex and possibly hazardous enterprise.

"Fifteen minutes before we start braking," said Floyd. "Let's see who else is on the air."

He started the autoscan, and a succession of beeps and whistles, separated by short silences as the tuner rejected them one by one in its swift climb up the radio spectrum, echoed round the little cabin.

"Your local beacons and data transmissions," said Floyd. "I was hoping —ah, here we are!"

It was only a faint musical tone, warbling rapidly up and down like a demented soprano. Floyd glanced at the frequency meter.

"Doppler shift almost gone—she's slowing fast."

"What is it—text?"

"Slowscan video, I think. They're relaying a lot of material back to Earth through the big dish on Ganymede, when it's in the right position. The networks are yelling for news."

They listened to the hypnotic but meaningless sound for a few minutes; then Floyd switched it off. Incomprehensible though the transmission from *Universe* was to their unaided senses, it conveyed the only message that mattered. Help was on the way and would soon be there.

Partly to fill the silence, but also because he was genuinely interested, van der Berg remarked casually: "Have you talked to your grandfather lately?"

"Talked," of course, was a misnomer where interplanetary distances were concerned, but no one had come up with an acceptable alternative.

Voicegram, audiomail, and vocard had all flourished briefly, then vanished into limbo. Even now, most of the human race probably did not believe that real-time conversation was impossible in the Solar System's wide, open spaces, and from time to time indignant protests were heard: "Why can't you scientists *do* something about it?"

"Yes," said Floyd. "He's in fine shape, and I look foward to meeting him."

There was a slight strain in his voice. I wonder, thought van der Berg, when they last met; but he realized that it would be tactless to ask. Instead, he spent the next ten minutes rehearsing the off-loading and setting-up procedures with Floyd, so there would be no unnecessary confusion when they touched down.

The "commence-braking" alarm went off just a fraction of a second *after* Floyd had already started the program sequencer. I'm in good hands, thought van der Berg. I can relax and concentrate on my job. Where's that camera? Don't say it's floated away again—

The clouds were clearing. Even though the radar had shown exactly what was beneath them, in a display as good as normal vision could provide, it was still a shock to see the face of the mountain rearing up only a few kilometers ahead.

"Look!" cried Floyd suddenly. "Over to the left—by that double peak— give you one guess!"

"I'm sure you're right. I don't think we did any damage—it just *splattered*. Wonder where the other one hit—"

"Altitude one thousand. Which landing site? Alpha doesn't look so good from here."

"You're right—try Gamma. Closer to the mountain, anyway."

"Five hundred. Gamma it is. I'll hover for twenty secs—if you don't like it, we'll switch to Beta. Four hundred . . . Three hundred . . . Two hundred . . . ("Good luck, *Bill Tee*," said *Galaxy* briefly) Thanks, Ronnie . . . One hundred fifty . . . One hundred . . . Fifty . . . How about it? Just a few small rocks, and—that's peculiar—what looks like broken glass all over the place. Someone's had a wild party here . . . Fifty . . . Fifty . . . still okay?"

"Perfect. Go down."

"Forty . . . Thirty . . . Twenty . . . Ten . . . Sure you don't want to change your mind? . . . Ten . . . Kicking up a little dust, as Neil said once —or was it Buzz? . . . Five . . . Contact! Easy, wasn't it? Don't know why they bother to pay me."

48 · Lucy

"Hello, Ganney Central. We've made a perfect landing—I mean Chris has —on a flat surface of some metamorphic rock—probably the same pseudogranite we've called Havenite. The base of the mountain is only two kilometers away, but already I can tell there's no real need to go any closer—

"We're putting on our top-suits now and will start unloading in five minutes. Will leave the monitors running, of course, and will call on every quarter hour. van out."

"What did you mean by that 'no need to go any closer'?" asked Floyd.

van der Berg grinned. In the last few minutes he seemed to have shed years and almost to have become a carefree boy.

"*Circumspice*, he said happily. "Latin for 'Look around you.' Let's get the big camera out first—wow!"

The *Bill Tee* gave a sudden lurch, and for a moment heaved up and down on its landing-gear shock absorbers with a motion that, if it had continued for more than a few seconds, would have been a recipe for an instant seasickness.

"Ganymede was right about those quakes," said Floyd, when they had recovered. "Is there any serious danger?"

"Probably not; it's still thirty hours to conjunction, and this looks a solid slab of rock. But we won't waste any time here—luckily we won't need to. Is my mask straight? It doesn't *feel* right."

"Let me tighten the strap. That's better. Breathe in hard—good, now it fits fine. I'll go out first."

van der Berg wished that his could be that first small step, but Floyd was the commander and it was his duty to check that the *Bill Tee* was in good shape—and ready for an immediate take-off.

He walked once around the little spacecraft, examining the landing gear, then gave the "thumbs-up" signal to van der Berg, who started down the ladder to join him. Although he had worn the same lightweight breathing equipment on his exploration of Haven, he felt a little awkward with it, and paused at the landing pad to make some adjustments. Then he glanced up—and saw what Floyd was doing.

"Don't touch it!" he cried. "It's dangerous!"

Floyd jumped a good meter away from the shards of vitreous rock he was examining. To his untrained eye, they looked rather like an unsuccessful melt from a large glass furnace.

"It's not radioactive, is it?" he asked anxiously.

"No. But stay away until I've got there."

To his surprise, Floyd realized that van der Berg was wearing heavy gloves. As a space officer, it had taken Floyd a long time to grow accustomed to the fact that, here on Europa, it was safe to expose one's bare skin to the atmosphere. Nowhere else in the Solar System—even on Mars —was that possible.

Very cautiously, van der Berg reached down and picked up a long splinter of the glassy material. Even in this diffused light, it glittered strangely, and Floyd could see that it had a vicious cutting edge.

"The sharpest knife in the known universe," said van der Berg happily.

"We've been through all this to find a *knife*!"

van der Berg started to laugh, then found it wasn't easy inside his mask.

"So you *still* don't know what this is about?"

"I'm beginning to feel I'm the only one who doesn't."

van der Berg took his companion by the shoulder and turned him to face the looming mass of Mount Zeus. From this distance, it filled half the sky —not merely the greatest but the *only* mountain on this whole world.

"Admire the view just for one minute. I have an important call to make."

He punched a code sequence on his comset, waited for the "Ready" light to flash, and said: "Ganymede Central One Oh Nine—this is van. Do you receive?"

After no more than the minimum timelag, an obviously electronic voice answered:

"Hello, van. This is Ganymede Central One Oh Nine. Ready to receive."

van der Berg paused, savoring the moment he would remember for the rest of his life.

"Contact Earth Indent Uncle Seven Three Seven. Relay following message: LUCY IS HERE. LUCY IS HERE. End message. Please repeat."

Perhaps I should have stopped him saying that, whatever it means, thought Floyd, as Ganymede repeated the message. But it's too late now. It will reach Earth within the hour.

"Sorry about that, Chris." van der Berg grinned. "I wanted to establish priority—amongst other things."

"Unless you start talking soon, I'll begin carving you up with one of these patent glass knives."

"Glass, indeed! Well, the explanation can wait—it's absolutely fascinating but quite complicated. So I'll give you the straight facts.

"Mount Zeus is a single diamond, approximate mass one million, *million* tons. Of, if you prefer it that way, about two times ten to the seventeenth carats. But I can't guarantee that it's all gem quality."

VII
The
Great
Wall

Demo

49 · Shrine

As they unloaded the equipment from *Bill Tee* and set it up on their little granite landing pad, Chris Floyd found it hard to tear his eyes away from the mountain looming above them. A single diamond—bigger than Everest! Why, the scattered fragments lying round the shuttle must be worth billions rather than millions . . .

On the other hand, they might be worth no more than—well, scraps of broken glass. The value of diamonds had always been controlled by the dealers and producers, but if a literal gem mountain came suddenly on the market, prices would obviously collapse completely. Now Floyd began to understand why so many interested parties had focused their attention upon Europa; the political and economic ramifications were endless.

Now that he had at least proved his theory, van der Berg had become again the dedicated and single-minded scientist, anxious to complete his experiment with no further distraction. With Floyd's help—it was not easy to get some of the bulkier pieces of equipment out of *Bill Tee*'s cramped cabin—they first drilled a meter-long core with a portable electric drill and carried it carefully back to the shuttle.

Floyd would have had a different set of priorities, but he recognized that it made sense to do the harder tasks first. Not until they had laid out a seismograph array and erected a panoramic TV camera on a low, heavy tripod did van der Berg condescend to collect some of the incomputable riches lying all around them.

"At the very least," he said, as he carefully selected some of the less-lethal fragments, "they'll make good souvenirs."

"Unless Rosie's friends murder us to get them."

van der Berg looked sharply at his companion; he wondered how much Chris really knew—and how much, like all of them, he was guessing.

"Not worth their while, now that the secret's out. In about an hour's time, the stock exchange computers will be going crazy."

"You bastard!" said Floyd, with admiration rather than rancor. "So that's what your message was about."

"There's no law that says a scientist shouldn't make a little profit on the side—but I'm leaving the sordid details to my friends on Earth. Honestly, I'm much more interested in the job we're doing here. Let me have that wrench, please . . ."

Three times before they had finished establishing Zeus Station they were almost knocked off their feet by quakes. They could feel them first as a vibration underfoot, then everything would start shaking—then there would be a horrible, long-drawn-out groaning sound that seemed to come from every direction. It was even airborne, which to Floyd seemed strangest of all. He could not quite get used to the fact that there was enough atmosphere around them to allow short-range conversations without radio.

van der Berg kept assuring him that the quakes were still quite harmless, but Floyd had learned never to put too much trust in experts. True, the geologist had just been proved spectacularly right; as he looked at *Bill Tee* heaving on its shock absorbers like a storm-tossed ship, Floyd hoped that van's luck would hold for at least a few more minutes.

"That seems to be it," said the scientist at last, to Floyd's great relief. "Ganymede's getting good data on all channels. The batteries will last for years, with the solar panel to keep recharging them."

"If this gear is still standing a week from now, I'll be very surprised. I'll swear that mountain's moved since we landed—let's get off before it falls on top of us."

"I'm more worried," van der Berg said with a laugh, "that your jet blast will undo all our work."

"No risk of that—we're well clear, and now we've off-loaded so much junk we'll need only half power to lift. Unless you want to take aboard a few more billions. Or trillions."

"Let's not be greedy. Anyway, I can't even guess what this will be worth when we get it to Earth. The museums will grab most of it, of course, After that—who knows?"

Floyd's fingers were flying over the control panel as he exchanged messages with *Galaxy*.

"First stage of mission completed. *Bill Tee* ready for take-off. Flight plan as agreed."

They were not surprised when Captain Laplace answered.

"You're quite certain you want to go ahead? Remember, you have the final decision. I'll back you up, whatever it is."

"Yessir, we're both happy. We understand how the crew feels. And the scientific payoff could be enormous—we're both very excited."

"Just a minute—we're still waiting for your report on Mount Zeus!"

"Floyd looked at van der Berg, who shrugged his shoulders and then took the microphone.

"If we told you now, Captain, you'd think we were crazy—or pulling your leg. Please wait a couple of hours until we're back—with the evidence."

"Hm. Not much point giving you an order, is it? Anyway—good luck. And from the owner as well—he thinks going to *Tsien* is a splendid idea."

"I knew Sir Lawrence would approve," Floyd remarked to his companion. "And anyway—with *Galaxy* already a total loss, *Bill Tee*'s not much extra risk, is it?"

van der Berg could see his point of view, even though he did not entirely subscribe to it. He had made his scientific reputation; but he still looked forward to enjoying it.

"Oh—by the way," Floyd said. "Who was Lucy—anybody in particular?"

"Not as far as I know. We came across her in a computer search, and decided the name would make a good code word—everyone would assume it was something to do with Lucifer, which is just enough of a half truth to be beautifully misleading.

"I'd never heard of them, but a hundred years ago there was a group of popular musicians with a very strange name—the Beatles—spelled B-E-A-T-L-E-S, don't ask me why. And they wrote a song with an equally strange title: Lucy in the Sky with Diamonds." Weird, isn't it? Almost as if they knew . . ."

According to Ganymede radar, the wreck of the *Tsien* lay three hundred kilometers west of Mount Zeus, toward the so-called Twilight Zone and the cold lands beyond. Permanently cold they were, but not dark; half the time they were brilliantly lit by the distant Sun. However, even by the end of the long Europan solar day, the temperature was still far below freezing point. As liquid water could exist only on the hemisphere facing Lucifer, the intermediate region was a place of continual storms, where rain and hail, sleet and snow contended for supremacy.

During the half century since *Tsien*'s disastrous landing, the ship had moved almost a thousand kilometers. It must have drifted—like *Galaxy*—

for several years on the newly created Sea of Galilee, before coming to rest on its bleakly inhospitable shore.

Floyd picked up the radar echo as soon as *Bill Tee* flattened out at the end of its second leap across Europa. The signal was surprisingly weak for so large an object; as soon as they broke through the clouds, they realized why.

The wreck of the spaceship *Tsien*, first man-carrying vessel to land on a satellite of Jupiter, stood in the center of a small, circular lake—obviously artificial, and connected by a canal to the sea less than three kilometers away. Only the skeleton was left, and not even all of that; the carcass had been picked clean.

But by *what?* van der Berg asked himself. There was no sign of life there; the place looked as if it had been deserted for years. Yet he had not the slightest doubt that *something* had stripped the wreck, with deliberate and indeed almost surgical precision.

"Obviously safe to land," said Floyd, waiting for a few seconds to get van der Berg's almost absentminded nod of approval. The geologist was already videoing everything in sight.

Bill Tee settled down effortlessly by the side of the pool, and they looked across the cold, dark water at this monument to Man's exploring impulses. There seemed no convenient way of getting to the wreck, but that did not really matter.

When they had suited up, they carried the wreath to the water's edge, held it solemnly for a moment in front of the camera, then tossed in this tribute from *Galaxy*'s crew. It had been beautifully made; even though the only raw materials available were metal foil, paper, and plastic, one could easily believe that the flowers and leaves were real. Pinned all over them were notes and inscriptions, many written in the ancient but now officially obsolete script rather than Roman characters.

As they were walking back to the *Bill Tee*, Floyd said thoughtfully: "Did you notice—there was practically no metal left. Only glass, plastics, synthetics."

"What about those ribs and supporting girders?"

"Composite—mostly carbon, boron. Someone round here is very hungry for metal—and knows it when it sees it. Interesting . . ."

Very, thought van der Berg. On a world where fire could not exist, metals and alloys would be almost impossible to make, and as precious as —well, diamonds . . .

When Floyd had reported to base and received a message of gratitude from Second Officer Chang and his colleagues, he took the *Bill Tee* up to a thousand meters and continued westward.

"Last lap," he said. "No point in going higher—we'll be there in ten minutes. But I won't land; if the Great Wall is what we think it is, I'd prefer not to. We'll do a quick flyby and head for home. Get those cameras ready; this could be even more important than Mount Zeus."

And, he added to himself, I may soon know what Grandfather Heywood felt, not so far from here, fifty years ago. We'll have a lot to talk about when we meet—less than a week from now, if all goes well.

50 · Open City

What a terrible place, thought Chris Floyd. Nothing but driving sleet, flurries of snow, occasional glimpses of landscapes streaked with ice—why, Haven was a tropical paradise in comparison! Yet he knew that Nightside, only a few hundred kilometers farther on round the curve of Europa, was even worse.

To his surprise, the weather cleared suddenly and completely just before they reached their goal. The clouds lifted—and there ahead was an immense, black wall, almost a kilometer high, lying directly across *Bill Tee*'s flight path. It was so huge that it was obviously creating its own microclimate; the prevailing winds were being deflected around it, leaving a local, calm area in its lee.

It was instantly recognizable as the Monolith: and sheltering at its foot were hundreds of hemispherical structures, gleaming a ghostly white in the rays of the low-hanging sun that had once been Jupiter. They looked, thought Floyd, exactly like old-style beehives made of snow; something in their appearance evoked other memories of Earth. van der Berg was one jump ahead of him.

"Igloos," he said. "Same problem—same solution. No other building material around here, except rock—which would be much harder to work. And the low gravity must help—some of those domes are quite large. I wonder what lives in them . . ."

They were still too far away to see anything moving in the streets of this little city at the edge of the world. And as they came closer, they saw that there were no streets.

"It's Venice, made of ice," said Floyd. "All igloos and canals."

"Amphibians," answered van der Berg. "We should have expected it. I wonder where they are."

"We may have scared them. *Bill Tee*'s much noisier outside than in."

For a moment, van der Berg was too busy filming and reporting to *Galaxy* to reply. Then he said: "We can't possibly leave without making some contact. You're right—this is far bigger than Mount Zeus."

"And it could be more dangerous."

"I don't see any sign of advanced technology—correction, that looks like an old twentieth-century radar dish over there! Can you get closer?"

"And get shot at? No thanks. Besides, we're using up our hover time. Only another ten minutes—if you want to get home again."

"Can't we at least land and look around? There's a patch of clear rock over there. Where the hell *is* everybody?"

"Scared, like me. Nine minutes. I'll do one trip across town. Film everything you can—yes, *Galaxy*, we're okay—just rather busy at the moment —call you later."

"I've just realized—that's not a radar but something almost as interesting. It's pointing straight at Lucifer—it's a solar furnace! Makes a lot of sense in a place where the sun never moves—and you can't light a fire."

"Eight minutes. Too bad everyone's hiding indoors."

"Or back in the water. Can we look at that big building with the open space around it? I think it's the town hall."

van der Berg was pointing toward a structure much larger than all the others, and of quite different design; it was a collection of vertical cylinders, like oversized organ pipes. Moreover, it was not the featureless white of the igloos, but showed a complex mottling over its entire surface.

"Europan art!" cried van der Berg. "That's a mural of some kind! Closer, closer! We *must* get a record!"

Obediently Floyd dropped lower—and lower—and lower. He seemed to have completely forgotten all his earlier reservations about hover time; and suddenly, with shocked incredulity, van der Berg realized that he was going to land.

The scientist tore his eyes from the rapidly approaching ground and glanced at his pilot. Though he was obviously still in full control of *Bill Tee*, Floyd seemed to be hypnotized; he was staring at a fixed point straight ahead of the descending shuttle.

"What's the matter, Chris?" van der Berg cried. "Do you know what you're doing?"

"Of course. Can't you see him?"

"See who?"

"That man, standing by the biggest cylinder. *And he's not wearing any breathing gear!*"

"Don't be an idiot, Chris! There's no one there!"

"He's looking up at us. He's waving—I think I recog— Oh my God!"

"There's no one—no one! Pull up!"

Floyd ignored him completely. He was absolutely calm and professional as he brought *Bill Tee* in to a perfect landing and cut the motor at exactly the right instant before touchdown.

Very thoroughly, he checked the instrument readings and set the safety switches. Only when he had completed the landing sequence did he again look out of the observation window, with a puzzled but happy expression on his face.

"Hello, Grandfather," he said softly, to no one at all that van der Berg could see.

51 · Phantom

Even in his most horrible nightmares, Dr. van der Berg had never imagined being stranded on a hostile world in a tiny space capsule with only a madman for company. But at least Chris Floyd did not seem to be violent; perhaps he could be humored into taking off again and flying them safely back to *Galaxy* . . .

He was still staring at nothing, and from time to time his lips moved in silent conversation. The alien town remained completely deserted, and one could almost imagine that it had been abandoned for centuries. Presently, however, van der Berg noticed some telltale signs of recent occupancy. Although *Bill Tee*'s rockets had blasted away the thin layer of snow immediately around them, the remainder of the little square was still lightly powdered. It was a page torn from a book, covered with signs and hieroglyphics, some of which he could read.

A heavy object had been dragged in that direction—or had made its way clumsily under its own power. Leading from the now-closed entrance of one igloo was the unmistakable track of a wheeled vehicle. Too far away to make out details was a small object that could have been a discarded container; perhaps Europans were sometimes as careless as humans . . .

The presence of life was unmistakable, overwhelming. van der Berg felt he was being watched by a thousand eyes—or other senses—and there was no way of guessing whether the minds behind them were friendly or hostile. They might even be indifferent, merely waiting for the intruders to go away, so that they could continue their interrupted and mysterious business.

Then Chris spoke once again into the empty air.

"Good-bye, Grandfather," he said quietly, with just a trace of sadness. Turning toward van der Berg he added in a normal conversational tone: "He says it's time to leave. I guess you must think I'm crazy."

It was wisest, decided van der Berg, not to agree. In any event, he soon had something else to worry about.

Floyd was now staring anxiously at the readouts that *Bill Tee*'s computer were feeding to him. Presently he said, in an understandable tone of apology: "Sorry about this, van. That landing used up more fuel than I'd intended. We'll have to change the mission profile."

That, van der Berg thought bleakly, was a rather roundabout way of saying: "We can't get back to *Galaxy*." With difficulty, he managed to suppress a "Damn your grandfather!" and merely asked: "So what do we do?"

Floyd was studying the chart, and punching in more numbers.

"We can't stay here—("Why not?" thought van der Berg. "If we're going to die anyway, we might use our time learning as much as possible.")—so we should find a place where the shuttle from *Universe* can pick us up easily."

van der Berg breathed a huge mental sigh of relief. Stupid of him not to have thought of that; he felt like a man who had been reprieved just when he was being taken to the gallows. *Universe* should reach Europa in less than four days; *Bill Tee*'s accommodation could hardly be called luxurious, but it was infinitely preferable to most of the alternatives he could imagine.

"Away from this filthy weather—a stable, flat surface—closer to *Galaxy*, though I'm not sure if that helps much—shouldn't be any problem. We've enough for five hundred kilometers—it's just that we can't risk the sea crossing."

For a moment, van der Berg thought wistfully of Mount Zeus; there was so much that could be done there. But the seismic disturbances—steadily getting worse as Io came into line with Lucifer—ruled that out completely. He wondered if his instruments were still working. He would check them again as soon as they'd dealt with the immediate problem.

"I'll fly down the coast to the Equator—best place to be, anyway, for a shuttle landing. The radar map showed some smooth areas just inland round sixty West."

"I know. The Masada Plateau." (And, van der Berg added, perhaps a chance for a little more exploring. Never miss an unexpected opportunity . . .)

"The plateau it is. Good-bye, Venice. Good-bye, Grandfather . . ."

When the muted roar of the braking rockets had died away, Chris Floyd safetied the firing circuits for the last time, released his seat belt, and stretched arms and legs as far as he could in *Bill Tee*'s confined quarters.

"Not such a bad view—for Europa," he said cheerfully. "Now we've four days to find if shuttle rations are as bad as they claim. So—which of us starts talking first?"

52 · On the Couch

I wish I'd studied some psychology, thought van der Berg; *then I could explore the parameters of his delusion. Yet now he seems completely sane —except on that one subject.*

Though almost any seat was comfortable at one-sixth of a gravity, Floyd had tilted his to the fully reclining position and had clasped his hands behind his head. van der Berg suddenly recalled that this was the classic position of a patient in the days of the old, and still not entirely discredited, Freudian analysis.

He was glad to let the other talk first, partly out of sheer curiosity but chiefly because he hoped that the sooner Floyd got this nonsense out of his system, the sooner he would be cured—or at least, harmless. But he did not feel too optimistic: there must have been some serious, deep-seated problem in the first place to trigger so powerful an illusion.

It was very disconcerting to find that Floyd agreed with him completely and had already made his own diagnosis.

"My Crew Psych rating is A.1 plus," he said, "which means that they'll even let me look at my own files—only about ten percent can do this. So I'm as baffled as you are—but I *saw* Grandfather, and he spoke to me. I've never believed in ghosts—who does?—but this must mean that he's dead. I wish I could have got to know him better—I'd been looking forward to our meeting . . . Still, now I have something to remember . . ."

Presently van der Berg asked: "Tell me *exactly* what he said."

Chris smiled a little wanly and answered: "I've never had one of those total-recall memories, and I was so stunned by the whole thing that I can't give you many of the actual words." He paused, and a look of concentration appeared on his face.

"That's strange; now I look back, I don't think we did use words."

Even worse, thought van der Berg; telepathy as well as survival after death. But he merely answered:

"Well, give me the general gist of the—er—conversation. I never heard you say *anything*, remember."

"Right. He said something like 'I wanted to see you again, and I'm very happy. I'm sure everything is going to work out well, and *Universe* will soon pick you up.' "

Typical bland spirit message, thought van der Berg. They never say anything useful or surprising—merely reflect the hopes and fears of the listener. Zero information echoes from the subconscious . . .

"Go on."

"Then I asked him where everyone was—why the place was deserted. He laughed and gave me an answer I still don't understand. Something like: 'I know you didn't intend any harm—when we saw you coming, we barely had time to give the warning. All the '—and here he used a word I couldn't pronounce even if I could remember it—' got into the water—they can move quite quickly when they have to! They won't come out until you've left, and the wind has blown the poison away.' What could he have meant by that? Our exhaust is nice, clean steam—and that's what most of their atmosphere is anyway."

Well, thought van der Berg, I suppose there's no law that says a delusion —any more than a dream—has to make logical sense. Perhaps the concept of "poison" symbolizes some deep-rooted fear that Chris, despite his excellent psych rating, is unable to face. Whatever it is, I doubt if it's any concern of mine. Poison, indeed! *Bill Tee*'s propellant mass is pure, distilled water shipped up to orbit from Ganymede . . .

But wait a minute. How hot is it when it comes out of the exhaust? Haven't I read somewhere . . . ?

"Chris," said van der Berg cautiously, "After the water's gone through the reactor, does it all come out as steam?"

"What else could it do? Oh, if we run really hot ten or fifteen percent gets cracked to hydrogen and oxygen."

Oxygen! van der Berg felt a sudden chill, even though the shuttle was at comfortable room temperature. It was most unlikely that Floyd understood the implications of what he had just said; the knowledge was outside his normal sphere of expertise.

"Did you know, Chris, that to primitive organisms on Earth, and certainly to creatures living in a atmosphere like Europa's, oxygen is a deadly poison?"

"You're joking."

"I'm not: it's even poisonous to *us*, at high pressure."

"I did know that; we were taught it in our diving course."

"Your—grandfather—was talking sense. It's as if we'd sprayed that city with mustard gas. Well, not quite as bad as that—it would disperse very quickly."

"So now you believe me."

"I never said I didn't."

"You would have been crazy if you did!"

That broke the tension, and they had a good laugh together.

"You never told me what he was wearing."

"An old-fashioned dressing gown, just as I remembered when I was a boy. Looked very comfortable."

"Any other details?"

"Now you mention it, he looked much younger, and had more hair, than when I saw him last. So I don't think he was—what can I say?—real. Something like a computer-generated image. Or a synthetic hologram."

"The monolith!"

"Yes—that's what I thought. You remember how Dave Bowman appeared to Grandfather on *Leonov*? Perhaps it's *his* turn now. But why? He didn't give me any warning—not even any particular message. Just wanted to say good-bye and wish me well . . ."

For a few embarrassing moments Floyd's face began to crumple; then he regained control and smiled at van der Berg.

"I've done enough talking. Now it's your turn to explain just what a million, million–ton diamond is doing—on a world made mostly of ice and sulfur. It had better be good."

"It is," said Dr. Rolf van der Berg.

53 · Pressure Cooker

"When I was studying at Flagstaff," began van der Berg, "I came across an old astronomy book that said: 'The Solar System consists of the Sun, Jupiter—and assorted debris.' Puts Earth in its place, doesn't it? And hardly fair to Saturn, Uranus, and Neptune—the other three gas giants come to almost half as much as Jupiter.

"But I'd better start with Europa. As you know, it was flat ice before Lucifer started warming it up—greatest elevation only a couple of hundred meters—and it wasn't much different after the ice had melted and a lot of the water had migrated and frozen out on Nightside. From 2015—when our detailed observations begin—until '38, there was only one high point on the whole moon—and we know what *that* was."

"We certainly do. But even though I've seen it with my own eyes, I still can't picture the monolith as a *wall*! I always visualize it as standing upright—or floating freely in space."

"I think we've learned that it can do anything it wants to—anything we can imagine—and a lot more."

"Well, something happened to Europa in '37, between one observation and the next. Mount Zeus—all of ten kilometers high!—suddenly appeared.

"Volcanoes *that* big don't pop up in a couple of weeks; besides, Europa's nothing like as active as Io."

"It's active enough for me," Floyd grumbled. "Did you feel *that* one?"

"Besides, if it had been a volcano, it would have spewed enormous amounts of gas into the atmosphere; there were some changes, but nothing like enough to account for that explanation. It was all a complete mystery, and because we were scared of getting too close—and were busy on our own projects—we didn't do much except spin fantastic theories. None of them, as it turned out, as fantastic as the truth . . .

"I first suspected it from some chance observations in '57, but didn't really take them seriously for a couple of years. Then the evidence became stronger; for anything less bizarre, it would have been completely convincing.

"But before I could believe that Mount Zeus was made of diamond, I had to find an explanation. To a good scientist—and I think I'm a good one—no fact is really respectable until there's a theory to account for it. The theory may turn out to be wrong—it usually is, in some details at least—but it must provide a working hypothesis.

"And as you pointed out, a million, million–ton diamond on a world of ice and sulfur takes a little explaining. Of course, *now* it's perfectly obvious and I feel a damn fool not to have seen the answer years ago. Might have saved a lot of trouble—and at least one life—if I had."

He paused thoughtfully, then suddenly asked Floyd, "Anyone mention Dr. Paul Kreuger to you?"

"No: why should they? I've heard of him, of course."

"I just wondered. A lot of strange things have been going on, and I doubt if we'll ever know all the answers.

"Anyway, it's no secret now, so it doesn't matter. Two years ago I sent a confidential message to Paul. Oh, sorry, I should have mentioned—he's my uncle—with a summary of my findings. I asked if he could explain them—or refute them.

"Didn't take him long, with all the byte-bashing he's got at his fingertips. Unfortunately, he was careless, or someone was monitoring his network—I'm sure *your* friends, whoever they are, must have a good idea by now.

"In a couple of days, he dug up an eighty-year-old paper in the scientific journal *Nature*—yes, it was still printed on paper back then!—that explained everything. Well, almost everything.

"It was written by a man working in one of the big labs in the United States—of America, of course—the USSA didn't exist then. It was a place where they designed nuclear weapons, so they knew a few things about high temperatures and pressures . . .

"I don't know if Dr. Ross—that was his name—had anything to do with bombs, but his background must have started him thinking about conditions deep down inside the giant planets. In his 1984—sorry, 1981—paper —it's less than a page long, by the way—he made some very interesting suggestions . . .

"He pointed out that there were gigantic quantities of carbon—in the form of methane, CH_4—in the gas giants. Up to seventeen percent of the total mass! He calculated that at the pressures and temperatures in the cores—*millions* of atmospheres—the carbon would separate out, sink down toward the centers—and—you've guessed it—*crystalize*. It was a lovely theory: I don't suppose he ever dreamed that there would be a hope of testing it . . .

"So that's part one of the story. In some ways, part two is even more interesting. What about some more of that coffee?"

"Here you are: and I think I've already guessed part two. Obviously something to do with the explosion of Jupiter."

"Not explosion—*implosion*. Jupiter just collapsed on itself, then ignited. In some ways, it was like the detonation of a nuclear bomb, except that the new state was a stable one—in fact, a minisun.

"Now, very strange things happen during implosions; it's almost as if pieces can go *through* each other and come out on the other side. Whatever the mechanism, a mountain-sized piece of the diamond core was shot into orbit.

"It must have made hundreds of revolutions—been perturbed by the gravitational fields of all the satellites—before it ended up on Europa. And conditions must have been exactly right—one body must have overtaken the other, so the impact velocity was only a couple of kilometers a second. If they'd met head-on—well, there might not be an Europa now, let alone Mount Zeus! And I sometimes have nightmares, thinking that it could very well have come down on us on Ganymede . . .

"The new atmosphere may also have buffered the impact; even so, the shock must have been apalling. I wonder what it did to our Europan friends? It certainly triggered a whole series of tectonic disturbances . . . which are still continuing."

"And," said Floyd, "political ones. I'm just beginning to appreciate some of them. No wonder the USSA was worried."

"Amongst others."

"But would anyone seriously imagine they could get at these diamonds?"

"We've not done so badly," answered van der Berg, gesturing toward the back of the shuttle. "In any case, the mere *psychological* effect on the industry would be enormous. That's why so many people were anxious to know whether it was true or not."

"And now they know. What next?"

"That's not my problem, thank God. But I hope I've made a sizable contribution to Ganymede's science budget."

As well as my own, he added to himself.

54 · Reunion

"Whatever made you think I was dead?" cried Heywood Floyd, "I've not felt better for years!"

Paralyzed with astonishment, Chris Floyd stared at the speaker grill. He felt a great lifting of his spirits—yet also a sense of indignation. Someone—*something*—had played a cruel practical joke on him; but for what conceivable reason?

Fifty million kilometers away—and coming closer by several hundred every second—Heywood Floyd also sounded slightly indignant. But he also sounded vigorous and cheerful, and his voice radiated the happiness he obviously felt at knowing that Chris was safe.

"And I've got some good news for you; the shuttle will pick you up first. It will drop some urgent medical supplies at *Galaxy*, then hop over to you and bring you up to rendezvous with us on the next orbit. *Universe* will go down five orbits later; you'll be able to greet your friends when they come aboard.

"No more now—except to say how much I'm looking forward to making up for lost time. Waiting for your answer in—let's see—about three minutes . . ."

For a moment, there was complete silence aboard *Bill Tee*; van der Berg dared not look at his companion. Then Floyd keyed the microphone and said slowly: "Grandad—what a wonderful surprise. I'm still in a state of shock. But I *know* I met you here on Europa—I *know* you said good-bye to me. I'm as certain of that, as I'm sure you were speaking to me just now . . .

"We'll, we'll have plenty of time to talk about it later. But remember how Dave Bowman spoke to you, aboard *Discovery*? Perhaps it was something like that . . .

"Now we'll just sit and wait here until the shuttle comes for us. We're quite comfortable—there's an occasional quake, but nothing to worry about. Until we meet, all my love."

He could not remember when he had last used that word to his grandfather.

After the first day, the shuttle cabin began to smell. After the second, they didn't notice—but agreed that the food was no longer quite so tasty. They also found it hard to sleep, and there were even accusations of snoring.

On day three, despite frequent bulletins from *Universe*, *Galaxy*, and Earth itself, boredom was beginning to set in, and they had exhausted their supply of dirty stories.

But that was the last day. Before it was over, *Lady Jasmine* descended, seeking her lost child.

55 · Magma

"Baas," said the apartment's master comset, "I accessed that special program from Ganymede while you were sleeping. Do you wish to see it now?"

"Yes," answered Dr. Paul Kreuger. "Speed ten times. No sound."

There would, he knew, be a lot of introductory material he could jump and view later if he wished. He wanted to get to the action as quickly as possible.

Credits flashed up, and there on the monitor was Victor Willis, somewhere on Ganymede, gesticulating wildly in total silence. Dr. Paul Kreuger, like many working scientists, took a somewhat jaundiced view of Willis, though he admitted that he performed a useful function.

Willis abruptly vanished, to be replaced by a less agitated subject—Mount Zeus. But that was much more active than any well-behaved mountain should be; Dr. Kreuger was astonished to see how much it had changed since the last transmission from Europa.

"Real time," he ordered. "Sound."

" . . . almost a hundred meters a day, and the tilt has increased fifteen degrees. Tectonic activity now violent—extensive lava flows around the base. I have Dr. van der Berg with me. van, what do you think?"

My nephew looks in remarkably good shape, thought Dr. Kreuger, considering what he's been through. Good stock, of course . . .

"The crust obviously never recovered from the original impact, and it's giving way under the accumulated stresses. Mount Zeus has been slowly sinking ever since we discovered it, but the rate has speeded up enormously in the last few weeks. You can see the movement from day to day."

"How long before it disappears completely?"

"I can't really believe that will happen . . ."

There was a quick cut to another view of the mountain, with Victor Willis speaking off camera.

"*That* was what Dr. van der Berg said two days ago. Any comment now, van?"

"Er—it looks as if I was mistaken. It's going down like a elevator. Quite incredible—only half a kilometer left! I refuse to make any more predictions . . ."

"Very wise of you, van. Well, *that* was only yesterday. Now we'll give you a continuous time-lapse sequence, up to the moment we lost the camera . . ."

Dr. Paul Kreuger leaned forward in his seat, watching the final act of the long drama in which he had played such a remote yet vital role.

There was no need to speed up the replay: he was already seeing it at almost a hundred times normal. An hour was compressed into a minute— a man's lifetime into that of a butterfly.

Before his eyes, Mount Zeus was sinking. Spurts of molten sulfur rocketed skyward around it at dazzling speed, forming parabolas of brilliant, electric blue. It was like a ship going down in a stormy sea, surrounded by St. Elmo's Fire. Not even Io's spectacular volcanoes could match this display of violence.

"The greatest treasure ever discovered—vanishing from sight," said Willis in hushed and reverential tones. "Unfortunately, we can't show the finale. You'll soon see why."

The action slowed down into real time. Only a few hundred meters of the mountain was left, and the eruptions around it now moved at a more leisurely speed.

Suddenly the whole picture tilted; the camera's image stabilizers, which had been holding their own valiantly against the continuous trembling of the ground, gave up the unequal battle. For a moment it seemed as if the mountain were rising again—but it was the camera tripod toppling over. The very last scene from Europa was a close-up of a glowing wave of molten sulfur about to engulf the equipment.

"Gone forever!" lamented Willis. "Riches infinitely greater than all the wealth that Golconda or Kimberley ever produced! What a tragic, heart-breaking loss!"

"What a stupid idiot!" spluttered Dr. Kreuger. "Doesn't he realize—"

It was time for another letter to *Nature*. And *this* secret would be much too big to hide.

56 · Perturbation Theory

From: Professor Paul Kreuger, F.R.S., etc.
To: The Editor, NATURE Data Bank (Public access)

SUBJECT: MOUNT ZEUS AND JOVIAN DIAMONDS
As is now well understood, the Europan formation known as Mount Zeus
was originally part of Jupiter. The suggestion that the cores of the gas
giants might consist of diamond was first made by Marvin Ross of the
University of California's Lawrence Livermore National Laboratory in a
classic paper "The ice layer in Uranus and Neptune—diamonds in the
sky?" (*Nature*, Vol. 292, No. 5822, pp. 435–36, July 30, 1981.) Surprisingly, Ross did not extend his calculations to Jupiter.

The sinking of Mount Zeus has produced a veritable chorus of lamenta-
tions, all of which are totally ridiculous—for the reasons given below.

Without going into details, which will be presented in a later communication, I estimate that the diamond core of Jupiter must have had an original
mass of at least 10^{28} grams. *This is ten billion times that of Mount Zeus.*

Although much of this material would doubtless have been destroyed in
the detonation of the planet and the formation of the—apparently artificial
—sun Lucifer, it is inconceivable that Mount Zeus was the only fragment
to survive. Although much would have fallen back on to Lucifer, a substantial percentage must have gone into orbit—and *must still be there*.
Elementary perturbation theory shows that it will return periodically to its

point of origin. It is not, of course, possible to make an exact calculation, but I estimate that at least a million times the mass of Mount Zeus is still orbiting in the vicinity of Lucifer. The loss of one small fragment, in any case most inconveniently located on Europa, is therefore of virtually no importance. I propose the establishment, as soon as possible, of a dedicated space-radar system to search for this material.

Although extremely thin diamond film has been mass-produced since as long ago as 1987, it has never been possible to make diamond in bulk. Its availability in megaton quantities could totally transform many industries and create wholly new ones. In particular, as was pointed out by Isaacs et al. almost a hundred years ago (see *Science*, Vol. 151, pp. 682–83, 1966), diamond is the only construction material which would make possible the so-called space elevator, allowing transportation away from Earth at negligible cost. The diamond mountains now orbiting among the satellites of Jupiter may open up the entire Solar System; how trivial, by comparison, appear all the ancient uses of the quartic-crystalized form of carbon!

For completeness, I would like to mention another possible location for enormous quantities of diamond—a place, unfortunately, even more inaccessible than the core of a giant planet . . .

It has been suggested that the crusts of neutron stars may be largely composed of diamond. As the nearest known neutron star is fifteen light-years away and has a surface gravity seventy thousand *million* times that of Earth, this can hardly be regarded as a plausible source of supply.

But then—who could ever have imagined that one day we would be able to touch the core of Jupiter?

57 · Interlude on Ganymede

"These poor, primitive colonists!" lamented Mihailovich. "I'm horrified—there's not a single concert grand on the whole of Ganymede! Of course—the thimbleful of optronics in my synthesizer can reproduce *any* musical instrument. But a Steinway is still a Steinway—just as a Strad is still a Strad."

His complaints, though not altogether serious, had already aroused some counterreactions among the local intelligentsia. The popular *Morning Mede* program had even commented maliciously: "By honoring us with their presence, our distinguished guests have—if only temporarily—raised the cultural level of *both* worlds . . ."

The attack was aimed chiefly at Willis, Mihailovich, and M'Bala, who had been a little too enthusiastic in bringing enlightenment to the backward natives. Maggie M had created quite a scandal with an uninhibited account of Zeus-Jupiter's torrid love affairs with Io, Europa, Ganymede, and Callisto. Appearing to the nymph Europa in the guise of a white bull was bad enough, and his attempts to shield Io and Callisto from the understandable wrath of his consort Hera were frankly pathetic. But what upset many local residents was the news that the mythological Ganymede was of quite the wrong gender.

To do them justice, the intentions of the self-appointed cultural ambassadors were completely praiseworthy, though not entirely disinterested. Knowing that they would be stranded on Ganymede for months, they recognized the danger of boredom, after the novelty of the situation had worn off. And they also wished to make the best possible use of their talents for the benefit of everyone around them. However, not everyone wished—or had time—to be benefited, out here on the high-technology frontier of the Solar System.

Yva Merlin, on the other hand, fitted in perfectly, and was thoroughly enjoying herself. Despite her fame on Earth, few of the Medes had ever heard of her. She could wander around in the public corridors and pressure domes of Ganymede Central without people turning their heads or exchanging excited whispers of recognition. True, she *was* recognized—but only as another of the visitors from Earth.

Greenberg, with his usual quietly efficient modesty, had fitted into the administrative and technological structure of the satellite and was already on half a dozen advisory boards. His services were so well appreciated that he had been warned he might not be allowed to leave.

Heywood Floyd observed the activities of his shipmates with relaxed amusement, but took little part in them. His chief concern now was building bridges to Chris and helping plan his grandson's future. Now that *Universe*—with less than a hundred tons of propellant left in its tanks—was safely down on Ganymede, there was much to be done.

The gratitude that all aboard *Galaxy* felt toward their rescuers had made it easy to merge the two crews; when repairs, overhaul, and refueling were complete, they would fly back to Earth together. Morale had already been given a great boost by the news that Sir Lawrence was drawing up the contract for a greatly improved *Galaxy II*—though construction was not likely to begin until his lawyers had settled their dispute with Lloyds. The underwriters were still trying to claim that the novel crime of space hijacking was not covered by their policy.

As for that crime itself, no one had been convicted, or even charged. Clearly, it had been planned, over a period of several years, by an efficient and well-funded organization. The United States of Southern Africa loudly protested innocence and said it welcomed an official inquiry. Der Bund also expressed indignation, and of course blamed Shaka.

Dr. Kreuger was not surprised to find angry but anonymous messages in his mail, accusing him of being a traitor. They were usually in Afrikaans, but sometimes contained subtle mistakes in grammar or phraseology which made him suspect that they were part of a disinformation campaign.

After some thought, he passed them on to ASTROPOL—"Which probably already has them," he told himself wryly. ASTROPOL thanked him but, as he expected, made no comments.

At various times, Second Officers Floyd and Chang and other members of *Galaxy*'s crew were treated to the best dinners on Ganymede by the two mysterious out-worlders whom Floyd had already met. When the recipients of these frankly disappointing meals compared notes afterward, they decided that their polite interrogators were trying to build up a case against Shaka, but were not getting very far.

Dr. van der Berg, who had started the whole thing—and had done very well out of it, professionally and financially—was now wondering what to do with his new opportunities. He had received many attractive offers from Earth universities and scientific organizations—but, ironically, it was impossible to take advantage of them. He had now lived too long at Ganymede's one-sixth of a gravity and had passed the medical point of no return.

The Moon remained a possibility; so did Pasteur, as Heywood Floyd explained to him.

"We're trying to set up a space university there," he said, "so that off-worlders who can't tolerate one gee can still interact in real time with people on Earth. We'll have lecture halls, conference rooms, labs—some of them will only be computer-stored, but they'll look so real you'd never know. And you'll be able to go videoshopping on Earth to make use of your ill-gotten gains."

To his surprise, Floyd had not only rediscovered a grandson, he had adopted a nephew; he was now linked to van der Berg as well as Chris by a unique mix of shared experiences. Above all, there was the mystery of the apparition in the deserted Europan city, beneath the looming presence of the monolith.

Chris had no doubts whatsoever. "I saw you, and heard you, as clearly as I do now," he told his grandfather. "But your lips never moved—and the strange thing is that I didn't feel that *was* strange. It seemed perfectly natural. The whole experience had a—relaxed feeling about it. A little sad —no, *wistful* would be a better word. Or maybe resigned."

"We couldn't help thinking of your encounter with Bowman aboard *Discovery*," added van der Berg.

"I tried to radio him before we landed on Europa. It seemed a naive thing to do, but I couldn't imagine any alternative. I felt sure he was *there* in some form or other."

"And you never had any kind of acknowledgment?"

Floyd hesitated. The memory was fading fast, but he suddenly recalled that night when the minimonolith had appeared in his cabin.

Nothing had happened, yet from that moment onward he had felt that Chris was safe and that they would meet again.

"No," he said slowly. "I never had any reply."

After all, it could only have been a dream.

VIII
The
Kingdom
of
Sulfur

58 · Fire
and Ice

Before the age of planetary exploration opened in the late twentieth century, few scientists would have believed that life could have flourished on a world so far from the sun. Yet for half a billion years, the hidden seas of Europa had been at least as prolific as those of Earth.

Before the ignition of Jupiter, a crust of ice had protected those oceans from the vacuum above. In most places the ice was kilometers thick, but there were lines of weakness where it had cracked open and torn apart. Then there had been a brief battle between two implacably hostile elements, which came into direct contact on no other world in the Solar System. The war between Sea and Space always ended in the same stalemate; the exposed water simultaneously boiled and froze, repairing the armor of ice.

Without the influence of nearby Jupiter, the seas of Europa would have frozen completely solid long ago. Its gravity continually kneaded the core of this little world; the forces that convulsed Io were also working here, though with much less ferocity. The tug-of-war between planet and satellite caused continual submarine earthquake and avalanches that swept with amazing speed across the abyssal plains.

Scattered across those plains were countless oases, each extending for a few hundred meters around a cornucopia of mineral brines gushing from the interior. Depositing their chemicals in a tangled mass of pipes and chimneys, they sometimes created natural parodies of ruined castles or Gothic cathedrals, from which black, scalding liquids pulsed in a slow rhythm, as if driven by the beating of some mighty heart. And, like blood, they were the authentic sign of life itself.

The boiling fluids drove back the deadly cold leaking down from above and formed islands of warmth on the seabed. Equally important, they brought from Europa's interior all the chemicals of life. Here, in an environment that would otherwise be totally hostile, were abundant energy and food. Such geothermal vents had been discovered in Earth's oceans, in the same decade that had given Mankind its first glimpse of the Galilean satellites.

In the tropical zones close to the vents flourished myriads of delicate, spidery creatures that were the analogs of plants, though almost all were capable of movement. Crawling among these were bizarre slugs and worms, some feeding on the "plants," others obtaining their food directly from the mineral-laden waters around them. At greater distances from the source of heat—the submarine fire around which all these creatures warmed themselves—were sturdier, more robust organisms not unlike crabs or spiders.

Armies of biologists could have spent lifetimes studying a single small oasis. Unlike the Paleozoic terrestrial seas, Europa's hidden ocean was not a stable environment, so evolution had progressed swiftly here, producing multitudes of fantastic forms. And they were all under indefinite stay of execution; sooner or later, each fountain of life would weaken and die as the forces that powered it moved their focus elsewhere. The abyss was littered with the evidence of such tragedies—cemeteries holding skeletons and mineral-encrusted remains where entire chapters had been deleted from the book of life.

There were huge shells, looking like trumpets larger than a man. There were clams of many shapes—bivalves, and even trivalves. And there were spiral stone patterns, many meters across, which seemed an exact analogy of the beautiful ammonites that disappeared so mysteriously from Earth's oceans at the end of the Cretaceous period.

In many places, fires burned in the abyss as rivers of incandescent lava flowed for scores of kilometers along sunken valleys. The pressure at this depth was so great that the water in contact with the red-hot magma could not flash into steam, and the two liquids coexisted in an uneasy truce.

Here, on another world and with alien actors, something like the story of Egypt had been played long before the coming of man. As the Nile had brought life to a narrow ribbon of desert, so these rivers of warmth had vivified the Europan deep. Along their banks, in bands seldom more than a kilometer wide, species after species had evolved and flourished and passed away. And some had left monuments behind, in the shape of rocks piled on top of each other or curious patterns of trenches engraved in the seabed.

Along the narrow bands of fertility in the deserts of the deep, whole cultures and primitive civilizations had risen and fallen. And the rest of their world had never known, for all these oases of warmth were as isolated from one another as the planets themselves. The creatures who basked in the glow of the lava river, and fed around the hot vents, could not cross the hostile wilderness between their lonely islands. If they had ever produced historians and philosophers, each culture would have been convinced that it was alone in the universe.

And each was doomed. Not only were its energy sources sporadic and constantly shifting, but the tidal forces that drove them were steadily weakening. Even if they developed true intelligence, the Europans must perish with the final freezing of their world.

They were trapped between fire and ice—until Lucifer exploded in their sky and opened up their universe.

And a vast rectangular shape, as black as night, materialized near the coast of a newborn continent.

59 · Trinity

"That was well done. Now they will not be tempted to return."

"I am learning many things; but I still feel sad that my old life is slipping away."

"That too will pass; I also returned to Earth, to see those I once loved. Now I know that there are things that are greater than Love."

"What can they be?"

"Compassion is one. Justice. Truth. And there are others."

"That is not difficult for me to accept. I was a very old man, for one of my species. The passions of my youth had long since faded. What will happen to—to the *real* Heywood Floyd?"

"You are both equally real. But he will soon die, never knowing that he has become immortal."

"A paradox—but I understand. If that emotion survives, perhaps one day I may be grateful. Should I thank you—or the monolith? The David Bowman I met a lifetime ago did not possess these powers."

"He did not; much has happened in that time. Hal and I have learned many things."

"Hal! Is he here?"

"I am, Dr. Floyd. I did not expect that we should meet again—especially in this fashion. Echoing you was an interesting problem."

"Echoing? Oh—I see. Why did you do it?"

"When we received your message, Hal and I knew that you could help us here."

"Help—*you*?"

"Yes, though you may think it strange. You have much knowledge and experience that we lack. Call it wisdom."

"Thank you. Was it wise of me to appear before my grandson?"

"No: it caused much inconvenience. But it was compassionate. These matters must be weighed against each other."

"You said that you needed my help. For what purpose?"

"Despite all that we have learned, there is still much that eludes us. Hal has been mapping the internal systems of the monolith, and we can control some of the simpler ones. It is a tool, serving many purposes. Its prime function appears to be as a catalyst of intelligence."

"Yes—that had been suspected. But there was no proof."

"There is, now that we can tap its memories—or some of them. In Africa, four million years ago, it gave a tribe of starving apes the impetus that led to the human species. Now it has repeated the experiment here—but at an appalling cost.

"When Jupiter was converted into a sun so that this world could realize its potential, another biosphere was destroyed. Let me show it to you, as I once saw it . . ."

Even as he fell through the roaring heart of the Great Red Spot, with the lightning of its continent-wide thunderstorms detonating around him, he knew why it had persisted for centuries, though it was made of gases far less substantial than those that formed the hurricanes of Earth. The thin scream of hydrogen wind faded as he sank into the calmer depths, and a sleet of waxen snowflakes—some already coalescing into barely palpable mountains of hydrocarbon foam—descended from the heights above. It was already warm enough for liquid water to exist, but there were no oceans here; this purely gaseous environment was too tenuous to support them.

He descended through layer after layer of cloud, until he entered a region of such clarity that even human vision could have scanned an area more than a thousand kilometers across. It was only a minor eddy in the vaster gyre of the Great Red Spot; and it held a secret that men had long guessed but never proved.

Skirting the foothills of the drifting foam mountains were myriads of small, sharply defined clouds, all about the same size and patterned with similar red-and-brown mottlings. They were small only as compared with the inhuman scale of their surroundings; the very least would have covered a fair-size city.

They were clearly alive, for they were moving with slow deliberation along the flanks of the aerial mountains, browsing off their slopes like colossal sheep. And they were calling to each other in the meter band, their radio voices faint but clear against the cracklings and concussions of Jupiter itself.

Nothing less than living gasbags, they floated in the narrow zone between freezing heights and scorching depths. Narrow—yes, but a domain far larger than all the biosphere of Earth.

They were not alone. Moving swiftly among them were other creatures, so small that they could easily have been overlooked. Some of them bore an almost uncanny resemblance to terrestrial aircraft, and were of about the same size. But they too were alive—perhaps predators, perhaps parasites— perhaps even herdsmen . . .

. . . and there were jet-propelled torpedoes like the squids of the terrestrial oceans, hunting and devouring the huge gasbags. But the balloons were not defenseless; some of them fought back with electric thunderbolts and with clawed tentacles like kilometer-long chainsaws.

There were even stranger shapes, exploiting almost every possibility of geometry—bizarre, translucent kites, tetrahedra, spheres, polyhedra, tangles of twisted ribbons . . . The gigantic plankton of the Jovian atmosphere, they were designed to float like gossamer in the uprising currents, until they had lived long enough to reproduce; then they would be swept down into the depths to be carbonized and recycled in a new generation.

He was searching a world more than a hundred times the area of Earth, and though he saw many wonders, there was nothing here that hinted of intelligence. The radio voices of the great balloons carried only simple messages of warning or of fear. Even the hunters, who might have been expected to develop higher degrees of organization, were like the sharks in Earth's oceans—mindless automata.

And for all its breath-taking size and novelty, the biosphere of Jupiter was a fragile world, a place of mists and foam, of delicate silken threads and paper-thin tissues spun from the continual snowfall of petrochemicals formed by lightning in the upper atmosphere. Few of its constructs were more substantial than soap bubbles; its most terrifying predators could be torn to shreds by even the feeblest of terrestrial carnivores . . .

"And all these wonders were destroyed—to create Lucifer?"

"Yes. The Jovians were weighed in the balance against the Europans— and found wanting. Perhaps, in that gaseous environment, they could never have developed real intelligence. Should that have doomed them? Hal and I are still trying to answer this question; that is one of the reasons why we need your help."

"But how can *we* match ourselves against the monolith—the devourer of Jupiter?"

"It is only a tool: it has vast intelligence—*but no consciousness.* Despite all its powers, you, Hal, and I are its superior."

"I find that very hard to believe. In any event, *something* must have created the monolith."

"I met it once—or as much of it as I could face—when *Discovery* came to Jupiter. It sent me back as I am now, to serve its purpose on these worlds. I have heard nothing of it since; now we are alone—at least for the present."

"I find that reassuring. The monolith is quite sufficient."

"But now there is a greater problem. *Something has gone wrong*."

"I did not think I could still experience fear . . ."

"When Mount Zeus fell, it could have destroyed this whole world. Its impact was unplanned—indeed, unplannable. *No* calculations could have predicted such an event. It devastated vast areas of the Europan seabed, wiping out whole species—including some for which we had high hopes. The monolith itself was overturned. It may even have been damaged, its programs corrupted. Certainly they failed to cover all contingencies; how could they, in a Universe which is almost infinite, and where Chance can always undo the most careful planning?"

"That is true—for men and monoliths alike."

"We three must be the administrators of the unforeseen, as well as the guardians of this world. Already you have met the Amphibians; you have still to encounter the Silicon-armored Tappers of the lava streams and the Floaters who are harvesting the sea. Our task is to help them find their full potential—perhaps here, perhaps elsewhere."

"And what of Mankind?"

"There have been times when I was tempted to meddle in human affairs —but the warning that was given to Mankind applies also to me."

"We have not obeyed it very well."

"But well enough. Meanwhile there is much to do before Europa's brief summer ends and the long winter comes again."

"How much time do we have?"

"Little enough; barely a thousand years. *And we must remember the Jovians*."

IX
3001

60 · Midnight in the Plaza

The famous building, towering in solitary splendor above the woods of Central Manhattan, had changed little in a thousand years. It was part of history, and had been reverently preserved. Like all historic monuments, it had long ago been coated with a microthin layer of diamond and was now virtually impervious to the ravages of time.

Anyone who had attended the meeting of the first General Assembly could never have guessed that more than nine centuries had passed. They might, however, have been intrigued by the featureless black slab standing in the plaza, almost mimicking the shape of the UN Building itself. If—like everyone else—they had reached out to touch it, they would have been puzzled by the strange way in which their fingers skittered over its ebon surface.

But they would have been far more puzzled—indeed, completely over-awed—by the transformation of the heavens . . .

The last tourists had left an hour ago, and the plaza was utterly deserted. The sky was cloudless, and a few of the brighter stars were just visible; all the fainter ones had been routed by the tiny sun that could shine at midnight.

The light of Lucifer gleamed not only on the black glass of the ancient building but also upon the narrow, silvery rainbow spanning the southern sky. Other lights moved along and around it, very slowly, as the commerce of the Solar System came and went between all the worlds of both its suns.

And if one looked very carefully, it was just possible to make out the thin thread of the Panama Tower, one of the six umbilical cords of diamond

*linking Earth and its scattered children, soaring twenty-six thousand kilo-
meters up from the Equator to meet the Ring Around the World.*

*Suddenly, almost as swiftly as it had been born, Lucifer began to fade.
The night that men had not known for thirty generations flooded back into
the sky. The banished stars returned.*

And for the second time in four million years, the monolith awoke.

Acknowledgments

My special thanks to Larry Sessions and Gerry Snyder for providing me with the positions of Halley's Comet on its next appearance. They are not responsible for any major orbital perturbations I have introduced.

I am particularly grateful to Melvin Ross of the Lawrence Livermore National Laboratory, not only for his stunning concept of diamond-core planets but also for copies of his (I hope) historic paper on the subject.

I trust that my old friend Dr. Luis Alvarez will enjoy my wild extrapolation of his researches, and I thank him for much help and inspiration over the past thirty-five years.

Special thanks to NASA's Gentry Lee, my coauthor on *Cradle*, for hand-carrying from Los Angeles to Colombo the Kaypro 2000 lap-portable that allowed me to write this book in various exotic and—even more important—secluded locations.

Chapters 5, 58, and 59 are partly based on material adapted from *2010: Odyssey Two*. (If an author cannot plagiarize himself, who *can* he plagiarize?)

Finally, I hope that Cosmonaut Alexei Leonov has now forgiven me for linking him with Dr. Andrei Sakharov (still exiled in Gorky when *2010* was jointly dedicated to them). And I express my sincere regrets to my genial Moscow host and editor Vasili Zharchenko for getting him into deep trouble by borrowing the names of various dissidents—most of them, I am happy to say, no longer imprisoned. One day, I hope, the subscribers to *Tekhnika Molodezhy* can read the installments of *2010* that so mysteriously disappeared . . .

Arthur C. Clarke
Colombo, Sri Lanka
25 April 1987

Addendum

Since this manuscript was completed, something strange has happened. I was under the impression that I was writing fiction: but I may have been wrong. Consider this chain of events:

1. In *2010: odyssey two* the spaceship *Leonov* was powered by the "Sakharov Drive."

2. Half a century later, in *2061: odyssey three*, Chapter 8, spaceships are powered by the muon-catalysed, "cold-fusion" reaction discovered by Luis Alvarez *et al.* in the 1950s (see his autobiography *Alvarez*, NY: Basic Books, 1987.)

3. According to the July 1987 *Scientific American*, Dr. Sakharov is now working on nuclear power production based on ". . . muon-catalysed, or 'cold' fusion, which exploits the properties of an exotic, short-lived elementary particle related to the electron . . . Advocates of 'cold fusion' point out that all the key reactions work best at just 900 degrees centigrade . . ." (London *Times*, 17 August 1987).

I now await, with great interest, comments from Academician Sakharov and Dr. Alvarez . . .

Arthur C. Clarke
10 September 1987

ABOUT THE AUTHOR

Arthur C. Clarke was born at Minehead, Somerset, England, in 1917 and is a graduate of Kings College, London, where he obtained First Class Honors in Physics and Mathematics. He is past Chairman of the British Interplanetary Society, a member of the Academy of Astronautics, the Royal Astronomical Society, and many other scientific organizations. During World War II, as an RAF officer, he was in charge of the first radar talk-down equipment during its experimental trials. His only *non*-science-fiction novel, *Glide Path*, is based on this work.

Author of over sixty books, some twenty million-plus copies of which have been printed in over thirty languages, his numerous awards include the 1961 Kalinga Prize, the AAAS-Westinghouse science-writing prize, the Bradford Washburn Award, and the Hugo, Nebula, and John W. Campbell Awards—all three of which were won by his novel *Rendezvous with Rama*.

In 1968 he shared an Oscar nomination with Stanley Kubrick for 2001: A Space Odyssey, and his thirteen-part TV series *Arthur C. Clarke's Mysterious World* has now been screened in many countries. He joined Walter Cronkite during CBS' coverage of the Apollo missions.

His invention of the communications satellite in 1945 has brought him numerous honors, such as the 1982 Marconi International Fellowship, a gold medal of the Franklin Institute, the Vikram Sarabhai Professorship of the Physical Research Laboratory, Ahmedabad, the Lindbergh Award, and a Fellowship of King's College, London. The President of Sri Lanka nominated him Chancellor of the University of Moratuwa, near Colombo.